Yes, Trent was still the same unpredictable, exasperating guy.

Then again, Prudence thought, running her fingers lightly over her lips, in some respects he was altogether different. Her lungs constricted with excitement and her breathing quickened as the memories of his kiss flooded her mind. Yes, she had to admit, Trent had changed. Now— much to her chagrin—he had quite the opposite effect on her than the one he'd had in the ninth grade.

The very thought of finding Trent the Terror… *sexy,* made her want to run screaming. In the darkness her cheeks grew hot at the thought of how she'd allowed him to kiss her. And how she'd allowed herself to respond to him.

Trent Tanner, for heaven's sake.

Dear Reader,

Happy Valentine's Day! Silhouette Romance's Valentine to you is our special lineup this month, starting with *Daddy by Decision* by bestselling, award-winning author Lindsay Longford. When rugged cowboy Buck Riley sees his estranged ex with a child who looks just like him, he believes the little boy is his son. True or not, that belief in his heart—and his love for mother and child—is all he needs to be a FABULOUS FATHER.

And we're celebrating love and marriage with I'M YOUR GROOM, a five-book promotion about five irresistible heroes who say "I do" for a lifetime of love. In Carolyn Zane's *It's Raining Grooms*, a preacher's daughter prays for a husband and suddenly finds herself engaged to her gorgeous childhood nemesis. *To Wed Again?* by DeAnna Talcott tells the story of a divorced couple who are blessed with a second chance at marriage when they become instant parents. Next, in Judith Janeway's *An Accidental Marriage*, the maid of honor and the best man are forced to act like the eloped newlyweds when the bride's parents arrive!

Plus, two authors sure to become favorites make their Romance debuts this month. In *Husband Next Door* by Anne Ha, a very confirmed bachelor is reformed into marriage material, and in *Wedding Rings and Baby Things* by Teresa Southwick, an any-minute mom-to-be says "I do" to a marriage of convenience that leads to a lifetime of love....

I hope you enjoy all six of these wonderful books.

Warm wishes,

Melissa Senate,
Senior Editor
Silhouette Books

Please address questions and book requests to:
Silhouette Reader Service
U.S.: 3010 Walden Ave., P.O. Box 1325, Buffalo, NY 14269
Canadian: P.O. Box 609, Fort Erie, Ont. L2A 5X3

IT'S RAINING GROOMS

Carolyn Zane

Silhouette
R O M A N C E™
Published by Silhouette Books
America's Publisher of Contemporary Romance

SILHOUETTE BOOKS

ISBN 0-373-19205-3

IT'S RAINING GROOMS

Copyright © 1997 by Carolyn Suzanne Pizzuti

Printed in U.S.A.

CAROLYN ZANE

lives with her husband, Matt, in the rolling countryside near Oregon's Willamette river. Their menagerie, which includes two cats, Jazz and Blues, and a golden retriever, Bob Barker, was recently joined by baby daughter Madeline. Although Carolyn spent months poring over the baby name books, looking for just the right name for their firstborn, her husband was adamant about calling her Madeline. "After all, Matt plus Carolyn equals Madeline." How could she resist such logic?

So, when Carolyn is not busy changing Maddie, or helping her husband renovate their rambling one-hundred-plus-year-old farmhouse, she makes time to write.

MISS PRUDENCE MACKELROY'S PERFECT GROOM CHECKLIST

Candidate: Trent Tanner

Please answer the following:

Of Marriageable Age: Yes X   No __
Lives in Town: Yes __   No X
Has Dark Hair: Yes __   No X
    If No, would candidate be willing to change?   Yes __   No X
Has Mustache: Yes __   No X
    If No, would candidate be willing to grow one? Yes __   No X
Has Green Eyes: Yes __   No X
    If No, would candidate wear contact lenses?   Yes __   No X
Gives Gifts: Yes X   No __
    Last Gift Received: Bouquet of stinging nettles and poison ivy
    Date: 9th grade!

Based on above criteria, would candidate make the perfect groom?
                                           Yes __   No X

Would you be willing to marry candidate anyway?   Yes X   No __
    Why? I've loved him my entire life!

Mrs Trent Tanner

Prudence Mackelroy Tanner

Mrs. Tanner

My husband, Trent Tanner

Chapter One

Prudence Mackelroy tightened the sash on her robe and shivered. The early-summer air had turned suddenly frigid and her usually cozy bedroom had taken on all the homey ambience of a frozen meat locker. Somewhere outside in the late-night shadows a summer storm was beginning to brew, causing a branch from a nearby fir tree to thump loudly against her roof. The old cabin-style duplex, where she'd been living for the past several years, creaked and groaned as it clung tenaciously to the craggy cliffs high above the Pacific Ocean.

As she tidied her room and prepared for bed, Prudence cocked a curious ear toward her window, and wondered absently if she should go check on the elderly couple who had recently moved into the other half of the duplex. Not that it was really necessary. The walls of the old building were paper thin. If anything was wrong over in Mr. and Mrs. Skinner's apartment, she would most likely know it by now. Simple force of habit had made her aware of older people.

Rain now ran in rivulets down the foggy French panes, and off in the distance she could hear the distinct rumble of thunder over the ever-present roar of the sea. Slippers slapping, she moved across the cold hardwood floor. Wiping at the beads of moisture that had gathered on the window with the sleeve of her robe, she cupped her hands against the glass and peered into the night. The fathomless black expanse of the ocean loomed on the horizon.

Luckily she'd reminded the night crew down at the Howatowa Retirement Center—where she worked as a nurse—to turn up the thermostat. It promised to be a cold one tonight. Some of the frailer, more elderly residents couldn't tolerate the rapid drops in temperature as easily as they used to.

Sighing, Prudence turned away from the driving rain and made her way back to the edge of her bed. There, she dropped to her knees for her nightly prayers. Her late father, Rev. John Mackelroy, had instilled the habit in her from the time she could say amen, and it was a ritual that gave her great comfort and peace amid the stormy trials of everyday life.

"God bless all my old friends, down at the retirement center," she began, a small smile tingeing her lips as their sweet time-weathered faces appeared in her mind. "And, Lord..." Prudence paused and listened as a clap of thunder resounded just outside her window. "If you could, please send our poor old town a miracle. Nothing fancy," she hastened to assure, not wanting to seem greedy. "Just a little something to get the economy moving again."

Her cheeks puffed as she exhaled heavily. The small coastal town of Howatowa, Washington, was having some severe financial problems. People had been moving out in droves because of the sluggish economy, ever since the big lumber mill had shut down last winter. She couldn't help but worry about those who had lived in Howatowa all their lives, raising families, building careers, making homes. And now, the town was dying.

Prudence knew that it would surely take an act of God to revive the little town. But that was all right, for Prudence had faith. Faith that one way or another, her prayers would be answered. They always were. No matter how inconsequential.

Some sooner than others, she thought with resigned patience.

"And, Lord, I know you're probably pretty tired of me asking for the same old thing, and I really hate to nag, but I'd sure be grateful to you if you could send me my future husband pretty soon. As you well know, I'd prefer one who has dark curly hair, a mustache, and deep-green eyes."

She had always admired men who wore a mustache, with dark curly hair and laughing green eyes. Just like her beloved father. So, she decided that as long as she was putting in her order for a husband, she may as well get one whose looks she liked.

"And if you don't mind, please hurry, Lord! I'm not getting any younger, here. I know, I know. Twenty-nine is hardly ancient, but by the time I meet the man of my dreams and we get married, well, there may not be enough time to have all the children I want."

Being an only—and quite lonely—child herself had convinced Prudence that she would love nothing better than to fill an entire pew every Sunday morning with a brood of her own. That was why she wanted a set of twins right off the bat.

"A boy and a girl, Lord," she whispered into her clenched hands. "MaryJane and John, named after my late parents." She thumped her feet on the floor to keep them from falling asleep. "I know that's probably asking for a bit much," she whispered somewhat apologetically, "so I'll happily settle for a simple husband."

Prudence knew that someone with dark hair and green eyes was already out there for her, looking forward to the day when they would meet and marry. Someone wonderful. Someone she would recognize the second she saw him. And oh, how they would love each other, she thought dreamily, allowing herself to enjoy the lovely picture for a moment.

It would be a one-of-a-kind love. The kind her parents had shared.

The wind began to howl and whistle as it forced its way

through the gaps in her window sash, bringing Prudence out of her reverie. Surely the answer to her prayer was right around the corner, she thought with confidence. She murmured a heartfelt ''Amen'' as the fir branch began to beat wildly on her roof.

He would come.

She just knew it.

She had faith.

That was why Prudence Mackelroy was not totally surprised when, with a terrible roar of thunder and a blinding flash of light, a man—complete with curly black hair and a mustache—crashed through her ceiling and landed, amid a shower of plaster, on her bed.

''Thank you, Lord,'' she breathed in awe, as she lifted her eyes and came face-to-face with the handsome personification of her own private miracle.

Chapter Two

Trent Tanner blinked and shook the plaster out of his eyes to better see the raven-haired beauty kneeling at the edge of the bed. She didn't look the least bit afraid. Yeah, he thought grimly to himself. She was good. Cool as a cucumber. Didn't look at all like the low-life extortionist he knew her to be.

"Are you alone?" he demanded in a hushed voice, looking around for her husband. He brushed the ceiling debris off his back and shoulders, then pushed himself to the edge of her mattress. Falling through the ceiling hadn't been part of the master plan and he knew if he was going to get out of this situation in one piece, he'd better move. One never knew about these land-scammer types. They might look like living dolls, but they could be violent. Her swindler husband could pack a gun.

"Yes, I'm alone," the angel murmured in an awed voice. Her eyes were sparkly and round as she drew her lithe body to its full height.

Trent couldn't help but stare at her for a moment in the dim glow of her nightlight. She wasn't acting at all the way he would have expected a criminal to behave. He would have thought she would be running, or fighting, or at the very least, calling for her old man.

Tearing his eyes away from this celestial vision, Trent glanced around. "Where is your husband?" he barked, backing away from her and tilting his chin over his shoulder to assess the direction of possible ambush.

Her smile faded and she drew her delicate brows together in a puzzled line. "My husband?" Her fuzzy slippers whooshed softly against the hardwood as she rushed to his side. "I'm not married," she hastened to assure him. "I live here alone."

Trent's eyes narrowed suspiciously. "What about Mr. Skinner?" he demanded.

"The Skinners live next door, in the other half of the duplex. In apartment 2. They just moved to Howatowa last week," she replied, then shrugged.

For some reason that Trent was too keyed up to analyze, relief flooded through him. The rosy-lipped, dewy-eyed vision that stood before him was not an extortionist. He was in the wrong apartment.

Good.

No.

Bad. He was *supposed* to be in the attic, above the Skinners' apartment, gathering incriminating evidence against the two con artists. Alone and undetected. Not bumbling into the bedroom of the girl next door. Unfortunately, the lightning and thunder had startled him, and the next thing he'd known, he'd found himself on the bed of one of the most beautiful women he'd ever had the pleasure of laying eyes on.

Ah. She was beautiful, yes, but could he trust her to keep her mouth shut? Another furtive glance around satisfied Trent that she was telling the truth. She was alone. Good. He knew he had some fast talking to do. Maybe, after she knew the reasons for his midnight amateur-detective escapade, she would agree to keep this little...accident under wraps.

As he perused her room, he could feel her watching him.

Smiling at him. It was unnerving. Why wasn't she screaming her head off? She almost looked as if she'd been expecting him.

For a moment, he toyed with the idea that she was some kind of good-time girl. Perhaps the fact that a strange man had just landed on her bed was nothing new. But, something in her face made him discount that idea—something sweet, something innocent, something vaguely familiar.

"I suppose you're wondering what's going on," he stated matter-of-factly, and turned in the shadowy light of her bedroom to face her.

"Not really. In fact, I was—" she began, but was interrupted by the doorbell.

"Are you expecting someone?" Trent asked, striding toward her front door.

"Not anymore, I guess," she answered, shaking her head as she followed him to her darkened living room. "I mean, now that you're here. It's probably just the Skinners from next door, coming to see what all the...commotion was about."

"The Skinners?" A grim muscle twitched in Trent's jaw as he reached out, grabbed her arm and pulled her close. "Listen," he hissed urgently into her ear, keeping her firmly at his side as he moved toward her front door. "I need you to go along with everything I say to these neighbors of yours. I don't have time to explain right now, but if you don't do as I tell you and follow my lead, there could be dire consequences. Got that?" Peering through the darkness, he cupped her face with the palms of his hands. "I swear by all that's holy, you can trust me, okay?"

She nodded mutely, her eyes widening a touch with confusion. "Okay," she agreed hesitantly.

Trent pulled the front door open to find her elderly neighbors standing huddled together on her front stoop, wearing bathrobes and worried expressions.

"Are you all right, dear?" the older woman asked in a

quavering voice. "We heard a loud crash, and decided to check it out."

Yeah, Trent thought grimly as he took in the wizened faces of the plump couple, they were good. They didn't look at all like the money-grubbing sharks that they really were.

Their ancient hound bumped into the wall as it snuffed the air and then, after a couple of rusty woofs, it fell back on its haunches and regarded Trent through tired, bloodshot eyes. Trent's gaze darted from the dog to the old man. The resemblance was eerie, he thought, pulling the young woman more tightly up against his hip, his fingers biting warning signals into the soft flesh of her upper arm.

"Uh—" the raven-haired beauty glanced warily up at Trent "—I'm fine. This man just fell—"

"Yes. She's just fine." Cutting her off before she could blow his cover, Trent smiled indulgently at the older couple, then down at the woman at his side before planting a hard kiss on those rosy lips of hers.

Okay, so it was kind of a stupid move, he admitted to himself as his lips moved over hers, but it was the only thing he could think of to keep her mouth shut at the moment. Besides, there was something hauntingly familiar about this sudden urge to kiss her senseless.

But, he'd analyze that later.

Right now, the warmth of her sensuous mouth was simply a means to an end. A decoy, of sorts. Although, he had to admit, this sleuthing business was becoming downright interesting. It might even have been enjoyable if there hadn't been so much at stake.

Unfortunately, there was probably more at stake here than he knew, at this point. Which was why he had to come up with a plausible reason for being in this building at this time of night. And, he thought—loving the way this woman responded to his touch—he had to do it soon. Aided by a surge of adrenaline, his mind landed on a solution and, with a su-

perhuman effort at self-control, he managed to tear his mouth
from hers and sound halfway convincing.

"I'm sorry for all the commotion," he murmured to the
Skinners, his voice loaded with sexual innuendo, "but I guess
we...uh,...just got a little carried away back there in the
bedroom."

The young woman gasped.

With his free arm, Trent gestured back to the open door that
led to her bedroom, and nodded at the plaster that lay scattered
across her comforter. "We were, uh, trying something new.
The light fixture gave way at a critical moment, if you know
what I mean," he hinted, still grasping her arm through the
silky-smooth sleeve of her robe in a firm, warning grip.

She gasped again.

"I'm sorry if we bothered you," Trent apologized once
more, and waving a casual goodbye, attempted to shut the
door.

Mr. Skinner leaned into the opening, lips twitching as he
scratched his shiny, balding pate. "You're about to lose your
mustache there, young fella," he whispered, a gleam of something long forgotten burning in his baggy basset-hound-type
eyes.

The young woman turned her glassy-eyed gaze up at Trent
and gasped yet again.

Damn. Trent reached up and sheepishly pulled off his fake
mustache. So much for his disguise. "Heh, heh." He laughed
and winked meaningfully at the unscrupulous pair. His mind
raced for a yet another plausible explanation. Think fast, his
brain screamed. No matter what, they mustn't discover that
he'd been spying on them. His Uncle Rupert's life depended
on it.

Besides, he didn't know these people. So what if they
looked old enough to be his grandparents? So what if Mrs.
Skinner looked like the Grandma on the cookie package? They
could be dangerous. Deadly.

"Oh, that. Uh, well, sometimes we like to wear costumes—'' he lowered his voice as he confided chummily to Mr. Skinner ''—to spice things up. Right, honey?''

Aghast, she stared at him in shock. ''Wh-wh-what?''

Mrs. Skinner exchanged raised eyebrows with her husband. ''All right, then. As long as no one is trying to break in...or anything...'' Both she and her husband peered past the young couple as if trying to reconcile this new version of their rather prissy neighbor. ''I guess we can stop worrying....''

''Thank you. Yes, you can. Good night,'' Trent said over his shoulder as he steered his ''woman'' back into her living room and kicked the door shut with his foot.

Prudence whirled to face what she was beginning to fear was not the miracle she'd ordered, and opened her mouth to give him a piece of her mind. How *dare* he lead her darling little neighbors to believe that she was swinging from the light fixtures with him—in a *costume,* no less! As if she would ever participate in such a ridiculous game with this...this—she glared at his broad, retreating back—*hooligan.*

Unfortunately, the hooligan in question wouldn't stand still long enough for her to tear his head off. He was too busy snooping around her apartment. Just who the devil was this fallen angel? she wondered angrily as she stormed after him, fury crowding into her throat like mercury rising on a hot summer day.

Definitely not the answer to her prayer, she decided as he snapped on one of her small living-room lamps and used the dim light to begin his search for heaven only knew what. And he was definitely not the father figure she'd envisioned for her twins, MaryJane and John. Perhaps she had somehow gotten her wires crossed with God. She never would have asked for someone as...well, as ill-mannered. Plus, she had distinctly ordered a man with a real mustache.

''Hey!'' Prudence cried indignantly, rushing toward her mystery intruder as he pulled a bookcase away from the wall that separated her apartment from the Skinners. ''What do you think you're doing? I'll thank you to put that back where you—''

"Shh." He scowled and, leaning forward, listened intently. Frustrated, he pushed himself away from the wall and rubbed the place where his shoulders joined his neck. "Can you ever hear what's going on next door?"

Eyes narrowed, Prudence planted her hands on her hips. She wasn't afraid of this Magnum P.I. wannabe. "For heaven's sake. Why on earth would I care what the Skinners are doing?"

Momentarily, he stopped his thorough investigation of her apartment and regarded her. Picking up one of her porcelain collectibles, he tossed it from hand to hand for a moment, then pointed it at her. "Have you ever heard your neighbors mention a company called Fantasy Investments?"

"No," she snapped, snatching the knickknack out of his hands. With tender care, she set it back down on its shelf. "I don't know the Skinners well at all. If you will remember, I told you that they just moved to town last week."

"I remember," he said. His voice was distracted as he turned and walked out of the room.

"In that case," she hissed, taking off after him, "would you stop rearranging my furniture for one darn minute and explain to me who you are?" Scowling, she reached up and dragged her long, curly black hair out of her face. "And while you're at it, tell me what you were doing up in my attic."

"Uh-hmm," he grunted, more to himself than anyone. Lifting her drapes, he took a quick peek outside before continuing his investigation in her kitchen.

"Uh-hmm, what?" Prudence shouted.

"Yes," the midnight intruder muttered as he strode out of the kitchen and back into her bedroom. "This could work," he said again, staring up at the hole in the ceiling. "Yeah, this could definitely work." Running a thoughtful hand over his face he reached up and pulled his black woolly cap off his thick, silky... *straight* hair.

Prudence felt her heart drop like a stale pound cake. The man not only didn't have a mustache or a moral fiber in his body, he was also...*blond!* Good grief. This was not what she'd ordered at all. Moving closer, she peered up into his eyes and discovered much to her growing horror that they were blue. Not laughing green eyes like Papa's. But *blue.* Teasing, mischievous, crinkly-at-the-corners...blue. Something familiar about those blue eyes gnawed at her as she studied him.

Oh, no.

Oh, dear merciful heavens, no.

No! Prudence felt the blood drain from her face, and groped for the edge of her bed where she landed as her knees buckled under her. This was no answer to her prayer. This was the scrawny, freckle-faced little hellion that had made her life a living nightmare back in grade school. No. God would never do this to her.

"Trent?" she managed to weakly gasp as she clung to the bedpost. *"Trent Tanner?"*

Chapter Three

Trent stopped dead in his tracks. Squinting through the dim glow of the bedroom nightlight, he curiously regarded the stunned woman who was clutching so tightly the post of her bed.

"Yeah?" was his wary response as he studied her in the half-light.

Finally, Prudence could tell recognition had dawned and a slow grin split his face.

"Prude? Prudence Mackelroy? Pruney? The preacher's kid?"

A surge of anger strengthened her flagging reserves. "Yes." She bristled primly, rearranging her flimsy old bathrobe to better cover her knees. It was obvious he hadn't changed a bit. Still the same cheeky brat that he'd always been. What on earth was Trent-the-Terror doing, crashing through the ceiling of her apartment?

Good heavens. She'd thought she'd seen the last of him when his father had been transferred to Seattle, back when they were in the ninth grade together—well over a dozen years ago. It had been the happiest day of her life. She remembered how she'd jumped up and down and cheered as she'd watched the Tanner family's moving van pull out of Howatowa. With Trent moving thirty miles away, she could relax. It had been proof positive, in Prudence's mind, that vigilant prayers were indeed answered. Because no one had wished Terrible Trent gone more than she.

"Well, I'll be damned," Trent breathed. Clearly astonished, he ran a hand through his silky golden hair, pushing it out of his eyes to better inspect her.

"Yes," she retorted vehemently. "You will."

He ignored her outburst with a grin, just as he had when they were classmates. "I never would have recognized you," he said, that cocky curve of his upper lip she remembered so well now gracing his mouth. The mouth that Prudence now knew had the ability to make her heart somersault crazily. The mouth that—growing up—she'd itched to slap silly on a semi-regular basis until the end of the ninth grade. "You've lost weight," he noted, his eyes assessing the changes in her body.

Prudence felt her face flare and was irritated that he could still get under her skin quicker than a thirsty mosquito. While it was true that she had been a little on the plump side in grade school, she had never been as bad as Trent had liked to tease. For the first time in over a dozen years, she felt her jaw tense and she began to grind her teeth. Oh, how he'd tortured her.

"Just what are you doing here?" she demanded, leaping off the edge of her bed to face him. "I thought you moved away years ago."

"I did." Trent nodded and crossing his arms over his broad chest, made himself comfortable against her dresser. "I teach high-school math up in Seattle. During the summers, I travel. This summer I had to come back to Howatowa and...well—" he ran a hand over his mouth "—check up on my Uncle Rupert."

"Ah, of course. And my attic would be the best place to begin," she said, her tone snide.

Trent's grin broadened, a spark of admiration lighting his eyes.

Prudence knew Trent's uncle very well. Just last winter Rupert Tanner had moved into the retirement center where she worked as a nurse. She had a soft spot in her heart for the crusty, slightly eccentric Rupert.

Too bad she'd always detested his rotten nephew.

Darting a quick glance at Trent, Prudence closed her eyes and tried to picture the scrawny monkey he used to be against the powerful man that lounged so casually against her bedroom furniture, but it was hard.

For he, too, had changed for the better. Much better, she admitted churlishly to herself. Growing up, she'd always believed that the mischievous, completely unruly boy would jump into a life of crime and ultimately land in jail somewhere.

Who would ever have thought he would end up teaching high school in Seattle? That is, of course, she mused—opening her eyes and allowing them to slowly travel over his athletic build—if he really was a math teacher.

"Well, he's doing just fine," she said snippily, referring to his uncle. "So feel free to pack up and—" she pointed dramatically north "—get back to Seattle." She knew that it was probably too much to hope that this would satisfy the incorrigible Trent. That he would get out of her bedroom. Out of Howatowa. Out of her life.

Arching a curious eyebrow, Trent looked at her with interest. His hands slid comfortably to his narrow hips as he settled in for a chat. "You know my uncle?"

"Yes." Prudence sighed and, gripping the tall bedpost, sank back down on the edge of her mattress. Getting the hardheaded Trent to take a hike would require nothing less than an act of Congress. She remembered well his persistence from grade school. "I am a nurse down at the retirement center where your uncle has lived since last winter. He's wonderful."

"Yeah," Trent agreed, a look of fondness crossing his face.

"The best." Then, just as quickly as it had come, the pleasant expression passed and a grim look of determination took its place. He pointed to the far wall of her bedroom. "That wall connects to the Skinners' place, right?"

Rolling her eyes, Prudence bounded to her feet and followed him across the room. "Listen, Trent," she retorted, now thoroughly fed up with this older version of her girlhood nemesis, "I demand an explanation. And, another thing," she ranted, leaping in front of his face as he scratched his head and stared at the ceiling, "how dare you lead the Skinners to believe that we were, uh…you know…" she stammered and lost steam as he slowly trained his arrogant gaze on her. Something fluttery took wing in her stomach as his eyes locked with hers in a challenging and blatantly sexy tangle.

With a great effort, she broke the grip and glanced away. Yes, he may have changed on the outside, but on the inside, he was still the same aggravating boy that had given her fits years ago. She watched in helpless disbelief as he pulled her antique mahogany bed away from the wall and gingerly picked his way over her plaster-covered comforter. Wedging himself into the space he'd made, he pressed his ear to the wall and listened for signs of life at the Skinners' place.

"Uh-uh," she squeaked impotently and pointed at his footprints. That comforter was new. She fought the sudden urge to march over and slug him. Although, she had to admit, from the looks of his muscular build, that wouldn't work the way it used to. She hated herself for noticing how handsome he'd turned out. Wow. All those freckles and cowlicks had smoothed out quite nicely.

She shook her head to clear it of such lunacy.

"Listen up, buster," she cried, climbing after him as modestly as she could, given the static electricity that had her robe crawling in bunches up her legs. She wobbled across the pile of dust that littered her bed to where he stood pinned against the wall and poked him on the arm with a furious finger. "You can't just fall through my ceiling, land on my bed, and start snooping around my apartment without any explanation!'' she shouted, then lowered her voice.

It wouldn't do to bring the Skinners running again, she thought, chagrined. No telling what Trent might get in his head to say to them next. Prudence shot a scathing look at his camouflage pants and black sweatshirt.

"Why the elaborate disguise?'' she demanded. Trust Trent to play Rambo in her attic.

Jumping back up on the bed, Trent steadied himself by grasping her shoulders and bestowed her with his usual insolent grin. "You're right. I know I owe you an explanation,'' he admitted and gestured up toward the hole that loomed over their heads. "Sorry about the mess. I'll be happy to fix it for you.''

"Yes. You will,'' she informed him in a clipped tone. "But first, you will explain it. Now!'' She gave the sash of her robe a savage yank to emphasize just how irritated she was, and nearly sent herself over the edge of the bed in the process.

Trent reached out and grabbed her arm to keep her from falling, and Prudence could feel the current of tension that radiated from his hand clear down to her toes. It was almost as if the lightning that flashed off in the distance had crackled between them. She could feel his uneven breathing on her cheek as he supported her. Time suspended for a moment, as they stared at each other, studying the changes that the years had wrought.

Then, a clap of thunder jolted them both back to reality, and Trent released her arm. Prudence shook her head slightly. What was happening to her? She had to get a grip on her thoughts. For a moment there, she'd almost wished that Trent would kiss her again. How bizarre.

He slowly ran a hand over his face. "It's a long story,'' he began before Prudence interrupted. "Maybe we should discuss it over a cup of coffee?''

"Oh, for heaven's sake.'' She sighed and kicked a chunk of her ceiling off her pillow and onto the floor. "Is this going

to take all night? Just get to the point. It's freezing in here."
She glanced up at the cavernous gap overhead and scowled.
"Now more so than ever."

A familiar twinkle lit his blue eyes. "Let's make some coffee. It will help you warm up. I take mine black."

"Argh," Prudence harrumphed, as she leaped off the bed
and stormed into her kitchen without so much as a backward
glance.

Ambling after her, Trent settled into one of her hard wooden
kitchen chairs and watched in amusement as Prudence—her
back ramrod straight in that prissy demeanor that used to make
him want to wrestle her to the floor—went through the mo-
tions of making a pot of coffee. Grounds flew, water sloshed,
cups clanked. If looks could kill, he would have been shaking
hands with Saint Peter about now.

He grinned. Funny how her pursed lips and darkly furrowed
brow still made him want to wrestle her to the ground. More
so now than ever.

Trent knew that Prudence probably didn't suspect that the
reason he'd given her so much grief in grade school was because he'd had a five-star crush on her. Of course, he would
sooner have died than admit he was crazy about the slightly
bossy, totally virtuous, completely feminine and cute-as-a-
button—chubby cheeks and all—preachers kid.

Back then, Prudence's larger-than-life dad, the Reverend
John Mackelroy, had scared the hell out of him. Although,
Trent reflected with a grin as Prudence haphazardly tossed
some spoons on a tray, that had probably been the whole idea.
The very thought of courting Rev. Mackelroy's pretty little
girl had struck fear into his heart, so he'd been content to
torture her every chance he got, instead. At least that way he
was getting some kind of a emotional response from her on a
regular basis.

Now, he could only hope that any ill will she might yet feel
toward him wouldn't interfere with his mission. Unfortunately,
if the jutting set of her chin was any indication, she was still

just the tiniest bit miffed. Oh, well. He sighed internally. She couldn't interfere. He wouldn't let her. If converting Prudence to his camp would further his noble cause, then he would do it or die trying. His eyes strayed to her hipline as it swayed fetchingly beneath her robe. Heck, he could think of a lot worse fates than going a few more rounds with good old Prude.

Convincing her that he wasn't just some screwup kid turned screwup adult would be tough, though. Next to impossible, actually, given their somewhat—his mouth curved ruefully— antagonistic history together. But, it would be worth it. For Uncle Rupert's sake.

Plus—he plunged his hands into his hair, dragging it away from his face—being that he still found Prudence as desirable as he had in the ninth grade made spending some time with her an interesting prospect. She was all woman now. And, he was looking at her through a man's eyes.

She was still just as pretty as he remembered. Prettier. Wild and curly, her raven hair was now shoulder length rather than the chin length she used to favor. Her face had thinned out a lot, revealing well-defined cheekbones that hovered delicately above those two deep dimples he remembered so well. Her lips were still bow-shaped, he noted—reflecting how they'd tasted back there at the front door a moment ago. And the deep-green eyes that snapped with life were older and wiser and somehow more beautiful than ever.

It was uncanny, the way she looked exactly like her parents. Same dark curly hair, same lively green eyes. He knew that Rev. and Mrs. Mackelroy had both passed away within the last two or three years. Everyone had said that once big John Mackelroy had died, MaryJane had missed him too much to carry on.

"I was sorry to hear about your mom and dad," Trent murmured, his voice low with compassion. "I know that's rough. My own dad died last year."

Prudence stopped, set the coffeepot down and turned to face

him. Her face grew emphatic as she seemed to forget her irritation with him. "Oh, Trent. I know. Rupert told me. I'm so sorry." She moved over to where he was sitting and slid the loaded tray to the middle of the table.

"Me, too." The pain of his loss was still acute. He could tell she understood. "It was his heart." Reaching forward, Trent retrieved his cup of coffee and plucked a cookie from the plate. "Luckily, he wasn't sick for too long."

"Mmm." Prudence nodded, taking the seat across from him. "That's good, at least."

No bigger than the average closet, the tiny kitchen held only a table and the two chairs in which they sat. The glow of the solitary bulb that burned in the old-fashioned fixture overhead lent a feeling of cozy intimacy. Outside the wind continued to howl, causing the light to flicker occasionally.

The tiny furrow in her brow dissolved somewhat as she said, "I always really liked your folks. How's your mom doing?" she asked conversationally and blew into her mug.

"Fine. Busy." The corners of his mouth quirked slightly as he leaned back in his chair. "She belongs to every social club for seniors that Seattle has to offer."

Returning his smile, Prudence took a sip of her coffee. "I remember she was on several of the committees at church here in Howatowa."

"Well, she's still at it." His eyes cruised slowly around her efficient kitchen, making mental notes, gathering data. "Nice place."

"Yes, well, it was a whole lot nicer before you decided to remodel my bedroom ceiling," she said sarcastically. The verdant light in her narrowed eyes took the sternness out of her words.

"I could install a skylight for you," he offered, tongue in cheek.

"No, thanks. I like it just the way it was." She smiled and looked around the room. "This place isn't perfect, but I'm partial to the way it hangs out over the ocean, clinging to the cliffs. Gives it a certain charm, I think. Besides, it's all I can afford on my modest salary as a retirement-center nurse. Jobs aren't exactly a dime a dozen here in Howatowa, if you haven't already heard.''

"I know. Rupert keeps me informed. He told me that practically half the town left when they closed the lumber mill last winter.''

Her eyes glazed over as she stared out the window. "It's so sad,'' she murmured to herself. "I just wish there was something I could do.''

"There is.'' Setting his coffee cup down, Trent leaned forward, his eyes steely with resolve as he trained them on her.

Prudence's gaze collided with his and she squirmed under his scrutiny. "This wouldn't have anything to do with why you were in my attic, would it?'' She sighed, her eyes narrowed skeptically.

"Everything.''

With this vehement word, the light overhead flickered once, then abruptly died as the electricity went out. They sat in the pitch-blackness for a moment, listening to the squall. A shutter flapped noisily against the side of the house and the wind wailed like an angry banshee.

For a brief instant the tiny room was illuminated by a flash of lightning and Trent was able to catch a glimpse of Prudence before the room was plunged into darkness once more. She looked worried. Thinking he would try to put her mind at rest, he reached out toward her with a reassuring hand.

"Aughh!'' Prudence shrieked in terror.

"What?'' Trent shouted. Her screams had spooked him.

"Something touched me,'' Prudence gasped, panting. "It...it felt...I don't know...like a big, scary...'' She groped for the word.

"Hand?'' Trent supplied.

"Yes! That's it! A big hand.''

"It was mine.''

"Oh.''

"I don't have hairy hands."

"Please, I said scary. And I'll thank you to keep your hands to yourself," came the prim reply.

"Aw, sheesh," Trent snorted in disgust.

Suddenly he was back in grade school, trying to do something nice for her, only to have it blow up in his face. Why did everything always backfire with Prudence? he wondered in irritation. It never worked that way with anyone else.

No. On a daily basis, he could help little old ladies cross the street, chop firewood for shut-ins, volunteer to coach the underprivileged and never once did any of these good deeds backfire on him.

"Where do you keep your candles?" he asked.

"Candles?"

Trent sighed. "You know, the little wax sticks with the wick on the—"

"I know what a candle is," Prudence snapped testily. Pushing her chair back, she stood and groped for the archway that led to the cooking area, only to fumble her way into Trent.

"Prudence?" he asked, as he pulled her fingertips out of his ear.

"Uh...what?"

"I think the big hairy hand is back."

She giggled in spite of herself. "My hands are not hairy," she said, mimicking him.

"Oh." There was a grin in his voice.

"I think I have some candles in my junk drawer," Prudence muttered, feeling her way out of her breakfast nook.

"I'll help you look," Trent offered, stumbling along after her.

Again, she laughed. "Look all you want."

Finally, Prudence located two utility candles and a book of matches, and soon had the little kitchen flickering with a warm glow. She handed him a candle and led the way back to the table. "Okay," she began, wearing that no-nonsense look on her face again. "Would you please be so kind as to tell me what's going on?"

Trent watched with interest as the flames danced in her eyes. Something in her tone told him that he could trust her with the whole story. It was uncanny how, out of all the people he could have dropped in on in the small town of Howatowa, Prudence was probably the most trustworthy.

"I'm trying to find out some information about your neighbors, and when I said 'This could work,' I meant your apartment is a perfect place to keep an eye on them."

"You mean spy?" Prudence frowned. "On the Skinners?" she asked skeptically. "Why on earth would you want to spy on that lovely old couple?"

"Because I have reason to believe they are running a phony land scam. They told Rupert and a bunch of his buddies down at the retirement center that they have plans in the works for a huge resort in Howatowa. Howatowa, for crying in the night, Prude. The deadest town this side of the Rockies. Not to mention that no one has seen these plans yet, or has even heard of this—" his expression was full of derision as he spat the word "—company."

"What company?"

"Fantasy Investments." Trent crossed his arms over his chest and snorted. "I ask you, what the hell kind of a name is that? As far as I can tell from the few inquiries I've made, they are selling resort property that doesn't exist. Then—" he nodded smugly "—I'll bet you a million bucks they're gonna take the money and run."

Prudence looked at him, certain, now, that he had lost what was left of his irritating mind. Oh, please, she thought. The Skinners? Why, they were a charming little old couple. And, they had a little dog. They were very, very nice.

"No," she protested. "I can't believe that." Prudence gave her head a vehement shake. "I've only known them a short while, but they seem so sweet. And why haven't I heard about this big resort they're planning to build?"

"You haven't heard the people down at the retirement center crowing over this golden opportunity? That's all they could talk about since I got here, two days ago."

Prudence swallowed. "I was on vacation most of last week." Shrugging, she took a sip of her coffee. "Actually, I left the day after the Skinners moved in next door. I took a cruise to Alaska."

Trent arched a teasing brow. "A cruise? On one of those singles love boats?" An unsettling twinge suddenly jabbed him in the gut. For some reason, he wasn't too keen on the idea of Prudence setting her course for adventure, or her sights on a new romance.

"Shut up," she groused. "It was a senior-citizens' cruise. I was checking it out for the retirement center."

"Ah." Trent hoped his relief wasn't too obvious. Now that he'd fallen back into her life and discovered that she was still single, he was glad that she didn't seem to have some guy in another port.

Sighing, she stirred some sugar into her coffee. "Besides, I had some time to use before our new director takes over." She looked morosely up at Trent. "Rodney Pillson—you remember him from grade school?"

Trent shrugged. "Vaguely. Wasn't he the one who was always wetting his pants?"

Prudence dropped her head dramatically on the table. "You would remember that. Anyway—" she groaned and lifted her head to look at him in the flickering light "—he was our last director. He packed his family up last month and headed to Seattle to take a job at a big seniors' center up there. Said there was no future in Howatowa for his kids. Who could blame him?" she lamented, grabbing a handful of her hair and twisting it into a loose knot at the nape of her neck. "So, I figured it was now or never for my vacation, considering I'll most likely be spending a lot of time during the next year, helping our new director get acclimated."

So, she'd been in Alaska all last week, Trent thought. That

would explain why he hadn't run into her down at the retirement center—he was quite sure he wouldn't have been able to miss her if she'd been there. His eyes flicked over her face and down to the gap in her robe that revealed the smooth hollow of her throat. She was definitely hard to miss. He pinched the bridge of his nose with his thumb and forefinger to forestall any further imaginings where her soft, well-worn old robe was concerned.

"Listen, Prudence, if you don't believe me about the Skinners and their crazy ideas, ask my Uncle Rupert." He allowed his hand to fall onto the table. "And some of his buddies. I'm telling you, Prudie, these little old people are on the verge of losing their shirts to this Fantasy Investments company. This kind of thing happens all the time. Older people are easy marks. Trusting. Like Uncle Rupert." He sighed, his face reflecting a certain protectivness. "Besides my mom, Rupert is my only living relative. I can't stand the idea of a great guy like him getting the shaft." His eyes glittered dangerously. "And, if I have anything to say about it, he won't."

Prudence nodded. Everyone in town knew Rupert was a typical old salt who always made his deals on a handshake. He was a man of his word, and believed that everyone else was, too. But still. The Skinners? Con artists? No way... She frowned. It couldn't be true....

"Well," she said, trying to explore plausible alternatives, "maybe the new resort is not a scam. Have you considered that possibility? Maybe this type of thing would be good for the Howatowa economy."

Trent's lip curled in disgust. "Yeah, it would be wonderful for *somebody's* economy, all right."

Prudence began to wring her hands under the table. She was suddenly very worried. Could Trent be right? Shivering, she reached for her coffee cup.

Mistaking her shivers for a chill, Trent leaned forward and took her icy hands in his, disregarding her order that he keep his hands to himself. "I don't suppose you could turn on the heat?"

"Unfortunately, it's electric."

"Oh." Trent ran the pad of his thumb over her knuckles. "How about if I build a fire? You're going to get pretty cold with no heat tonight." And no husband to keep you warm, he noted pleasantly to himself. "That storm looks like it's going to be here awhile before it runs out of steam."

With a grateful look, Prudence nodded. Picking up the flickering candles, she led Trent into her living room and settled herself in the corner of her shabby sofa. Huddling beneath a wool blanket, she watched him build a fire in the old stone fireplace and contemplated what he'd told her.

Could he be on to something, here? It was so hard to believe. The Skinners seemed like wonderful people. But then, she had to admit that she didn't know her new neighbors well at all. Before tonight, she'd only laid eyes on them twice. They tended to keep to themselves. Of course, she hadn't been home much since they'd moved in. It would take time to forge a neighborly relationship.

However, if what Trent said was true, that would account for their rather private life-style. Their little dog did seem kind of...well, antisocial. And that Mr. Skinner. Come to think of it, those bloodshot eyes of his were kind of...evil. She'd caught the lewd look he'd given Trent when he'd thought they were wearing kinky sex costumes. Prudence shuddered with revulsion, even as the fire began to warm her body.

Trent rocked back on his haunches and poked at the now roaring fire. Through the slits of her sleepy eyes, Prudence took the opportunity to study the changes that had taken place in him.

He was a man now. Virile, powerful, sexy. A ghost of a smile played on her lips. Who would ever have thought? Trent Tanner was a hunk. The merrily crackling fire backlit his strong profile, and Prudence felt a yearning in her belly for something that she couldn't identify.

Oh, for heaven's sake. What was happening to her? She knew what she wanted out of life. And the blond-haired, blue-eyed Trent Tanner was most definitely not it. She had a plan. She would stick to it. Someday, she would have twins with emerald-green eyes and curly black hair, she reminded herself.

Still, it certainly couldn't hurt to enjoy the way Trent's shirt molded so snugly to his impressive physique. The way his biceps bulged beneath the sleeves. And the way those silly camouflage pants of his hugged his well-muscled thighs and narrow hips. No, she decided, snuggling deeper beneath the blanket, looking was okay. She just wouldn't touch.

She had to stop thinking this way.

"What tipped you off?" she wondered aloud, in an effort to switch channels in her mind.

"Hmm?" Trent drew his gaze away from the fire and focused it on Prudence.

"How did you find out that the Skinners might be... swindlers?"

Shrugging, Trent stood and stretched before sinking down on the opposite end of Prudence's sofa and resting his legs on her coffee table. He lifted the excess wad of wool blanket from where it lay between them and pulled it across his lap and up over his chest.

"I guess I got suspicious when Mr. and Mrs. Skinner—under the guise of Fantasy Investments—notified Uncle Rupert that he'd won a mansion up on Howatowa Hill." He lolled his head on the back of the sofa to face her. "You know the one, Prudie, the one that all us kids used to say was haunted?"

"Uh-hmm." She nodded, her face scrunched in disbelief. "Uncle Rupert won that old relic? I can't even believe it's still standing."

Trent smirked. "Part of their marketing ploy. To get old folks excited about buying shares in the Fantasy Investments resort." He drew his legs up under him and leaned against the arm of the sofa, facing her.

Her brow furrowed as she contemplated his words. "Marketing ploy?" she queried.

Trent nodded slowly. "Yes. What better way to draw attention to their project than to kick it off by giving away a 'mansion'? It's a great way to get people involved and excited. Makes it much easier to talk to them about investing in this glamorous once-in-a-lifetime opportunity. Supposedly, all Uncle Rupert has to do is send a yet-to-be-disclosed amount of money to cover the taxes and transaction costs. Personally, I think somebody should pay Rupert to blow the place up. However, needless to say, Uncle Rupert can't believe his good fortune and is thrilled, buying the whole story, hook, line and swindle. Right now, he's anxiously awaiting further instruction so that he can take possession of his new...mansion.''

"Oh, dear." Prudence closed her eyes and groaned. It was worse than she'd thought.

"Yep." Sighing, Trent gazed toward the fire and his eyes followed the sparks as they swirled up the chimney with the hollow, whistling wind. "Call me a skeptic, but I just want to make sure these people—" he nodded toward the wall that separated the neighboring apartment "—are on the up and up, before Uncle Rupert and his buddies lose their shirts. So far, I've only been able to glean bits and pieces of the whole story from Rupert. He's a very proud man. If he even thought I was checking up on him, there would be hell to pay. I've tried to worm out more information about Fantasy Investments and his new mansion, but he's been pretty tight-lipped."

Prudence frowned. "Why don't you just go to the police?"

"Because I only have a gut feeling. Nothing concrete...yet. The cops don't have time to waste on my gut feelings. That's why I'm snooping around. I need proof."

Tightly hugging her knees, Prudence stared at the fire and hated the fact that Trent was making perfect sense. Even his nutty escapade in her attic was beginning to seem sane.

This was dangerous, letting Trent Tanner lull her into a false sense of camaraderie with him. In the past, the only thing being nice to Trent had done for her was land her in a heap of trouble. Lifting her eyes, she arched a skeptical brow. "I don't think you're giving your uncle any credit. If it was me, I'd just tell Rupert my suspicions."

Trent smiled tiredly. "Obviously, you don't know how hardheaded my uncle can be. Once he makes up his mind that you are a good person, and that what you're offering is a good deal—" he shrugged "—no matter how much evidence points to the contrary, he would give you the shirt off his back. That's why I wore the disguise. I don't want the Skinners to know that I've been spying on behalf of my uncle. It might put him at risk. But—" he grinned devilishly "—I don't have to worry about them getting that idea anymore, now that they think I have a legitimate reason to be here, do I, dearest?"

Narrowing her eyes, she sat up straight and scowled at him. "I'll never forgive you for that mortifying lie. You let them think I'm some kind of—" Prudence paused and grimaced "—tramp. For pity's sake, Trent. What if they're honest?" she argued plaintively, furious with him all over again. "I still have to live in this town."

"They might be," he admitted, but shook his head doubtfully. "I just think it's more than a little strange that my uncle suddenly wins an ancient mansion. A *mansion,* for crying out loud. Not a car. Not a trip. Plus, he didn't even enter a contest. The whole thing just smacks of a scam."

As much as it grated, she knew he had a point. "What did you hope to discover by crawling around in my attic?" she asked grumpily.

"I don't know what I'm looking for at this point. Shoot, I'm no Hardy boy." Lifting both hands, he threaded them through his hair. "I'm just trying to gather information now. I'll put the pieces of the puzzle together later. I guess I was hoping to overhear something incriminating in their conversation."

Worries of all sorts crowded into Prudence's throat. This was just awful. Only an hour ago she'd been peacefully asking for answers to her prayers, and now… Well, now her orderly, apple-pie life had become a victim of Hurricane Trent. Questions whirled unanswered in her mind, driving her half crazy with fear.

Were her neighbors really swindlers? Was the resort a scam? Had her dear little friends down at the retirement center lost their money? And last but certainly not least, was Trent the answer to her prayers?

Oh, good grief. The last question was too horrible to contemplate. It was all too much. Tossing off the blanket, she leaped to her feet and began to poke at the fire with a piece of kindling.

Taking her movements as his cue to leave, Trent stood and folded the blanket. "I gotta get going, Prudie, but I'll be back tomorrow to fix your ceiling. It's probably going to take several evenings to fix, but that's perfect. Maybe while I'm up there, I can pick up a clue or two."

Prudence stopped prodding the flaming logs and glanced into her bedroom at the gaping hole over her bed. The idea that Trent would be spending several evenings in her home both terrified and excited her. What was it about Trent that brought out the split personality in her? One minute she wanted to run her fingers through his thick golden hair, and the next minute, she wanted to tear it out. No one else could make her act like such a complete lunatic. She had to set some ground rules with him. It was her only hope.

"Trent," she called as he moved toward her front door.

"Yeah?"

Clasping her robe together at her throat, she narrowed her eyes at him. "Listen, I want to make it clear that I don't appreciate your telling people that we are…uh…"

"Intimate?" He raised a lazy eyebrow, and allowed his gaze to drop to where her hands clutched her robe.

How could the man send her blood pressure skyrocketing up the chimney with one lousy word?

"Whatever," she replied huffily. "Everyone knows that I

would never become...involved that way with a rapscallion such as yourself, Trent Tanner." Gracious, she thought, wincing internally as she listened to herself. She hadn't gone on like such a stuffy little prig since the ninth grade. "The man I give myself to, will be... He will be..." Why was she telling him this? "Ethical, kind, loving, and he will have dark curly hair and green eyes, and a real mustache," she declared, suddenly back in grade school and feeling like the totally prissy, uptight dork that she was sure he thought she was.

"Yeah?" he drawled lazily.

"Yeah! And, I have faith that someday he will come into my life and we will marry. Until that day, however, I would appreciate it if you would not sully my reputation."

"Sully?" His grin was arrogant as he scratched his silky blond head.

She stuffed her hands into her pockets to keep from leaping across the room and trying to strangle him. He was doing it to her again. Forcing her into the role of Miss Goody Two-Shoes.

"Trent, I have no doubt that you have not changed one iota since the ninth grade. Back then, you made my life a living hell...."

The lights chose that moment to flare to life, revealing Prudence's flushed cheeks and dagger-shooting eyes. She blinked rapidly in the sudden brightness.

"Careful there, Prudie," Trent cautioned. "I don't want to be held eternally responsible for your, uh, spicy vocabulary."

Prudence seethed. "And you continue to do so to this very day." She pointed to the door. "I think it's time that you left now." Darn. Why had things degenerated this way? Just like the old days. He would get under her skin, she would yell. And things had gone so nicely for a few minutes, there. She should have known better than to believe that she could have a normal, adult relationship with Trent.

Yanking his dark woolly cap back onto his golden mop of hair, Trent strode to her front door and grasped the doorknob.

"Happy to," he said, wiggling his eyebrows at her. "However, in the best interests of the entire community of Howatowa, I think the Skinners should continue to believe that we are an…item. And, while I fix your ceiling, your apartment is the perfect place for me to get a bead on their comings and goings over the next few days. Don't worry," he assured her, "your chastity is safe with me." He leered wolfishly. "Unless of course, the Skinners are watching."

He flung the front door open and noticed that the lights were back on in the old couple's apartment. They could be up. They could be watching. What the heck? he thought recklessly, reaching back into Prudence's apartment and hauling her out onto the stoop with him.

Dragging her into his arms, he lowered his mouth to hers once again, for a kiss that robbed his lungs of precious oxygen. Man. It was just as good as he'd always dreamed it would be, back when they were kids. Better. Her mouth was unbelievably sweet and, for someone who was busy waiting for the answer to her prayer to come along and sweep her off her feet, she kissed like a maniac. Damn. As much as he would like to pretend that he was doing this for the benefit of the con artists next door, and for the welfare of the town of Howatowa in general, he knew it wasn't true.

Trent Tanner was kissing Prudence Mackelroy because, for most of his adolescence, he'd wondered what it would be like. And now he knew. It was heavenly. Abruptly, he ended their mind-numbing kiss and let her go.

She stood, looking decidedly bewildered as he moved across the porch.

"Goodbye, babe," he shouted rakishly over his shoulder, hoping that the Skinners could hear. "I'll be back tomorrow to get some work done…in the bedroom."

"Oof," Prudence cried, and rushing back into her now warm apartment, slammed the door.

Chapter Four

Later that night, after vacuuming her pillows and changing the sheets, Prudence lay in her bed staring through the darkened shadows at the hole in her ceiling—and thinking about Trent. Trust Trent Tanner to make a flamboyant, completely idiotic reentrance into her life.

Of course, why such outrageous behavior on his part should surprise her, she would never know. Back in grade school, he'd always been attempting some daredevil, attention-getting-type stunt that had threatened to permanently straighten her wildly curly hair.

Closing her eyes, she allowed her mind to drift back to the time in sixth grade, when Trent had brought a skunk to school for show-and-tell. He'd told her it was a polecat, she recalled with a tiny smile as she pulled her blankets up under her chin. She should have known better than to try and pet the exotic-looking feline with the fetching white stripe. Her father was none too pleased at having to bury one of her favorite dresses along with her shoes and socks.

And worst of all, her mother had chopped off her long, glorious hair and insisted that she wear her it chin-length from then on. Prudence winced at the memory. It hadn't been a good look, what with her plump, apple cheeks. Short like that, it tended to spring in unruly ringlets from her head—especially in the Pacific Ocean's winter mist—bringing to mind a young Shirley Temple after a tussle with an electric eel.

Images of Trent tugging on her coils and watching with boyish delight as they sprang back at her head swam once again in her mind. The fact that he made fun of her only added insult to injury, considering it was his darn fault that she had to wear her hair in that hideous style in the first place.

She sighed heavily. It seemed that every year had had its shining moments with Trent. In the seventh grade, she remembered the time he'd brought her a bouquet of wildflowers to make up for some heinous crime or other he'd committed against her. She'd been on the verge of forgiving him until she realized the bouquet was composed largely of poison oak and stinging nettle. After the nurse had excused her from class for the rest of the day, she'd gone home and spent the entire afternoon tingling, itching, and plotting revenge.

And of course, who could forget the fateful day in ninth grade when she'd discovered a skinned hogshead that he'd swiped from the butcher shop in her backpack during biology lab? Some people liked to say that her screams of terror could still be heard ringing in the Howatowa hills. She certainly hadn't wanted him as a lab partner. That had been his idea.

There were other outlandish events, far too numerous to even remember. All examples of Trent's penchant for crazy stunts—crazy stunts that had the strange habit of backfiring in her direction.

Obviously, she huffed to herself, as she searched for a comfortable position under her stained and soiled comforter, nothing had changed.

"Why, Lord?" she whispered up toward the newly opened entrance to her attic. "Why me?"

Yes, Trent was still the same rowdy delinquent he ever was. Then again, she thought, running her fingers lightly over her lips, in some respects he was altogether different. Her lungs constricted with excitement and her breathing quickened as the memories of his parting kiss flooded her mind. Yes, she had to admit, in some respects Trent had changed. Now—much to her chagrin—he had quite the opposite effect on her to the one he'd had in the ninth grade.

The very thought of finding the freckle-faced Trent-the-Terror...sexy, made her want to run screaming over the sheer cliffs in her backyard and into the ocean. In the darkness, her cheeks grew hot at the thought of how she'd allowed him to kiss her out on the front porch. And how she'd allowed herself to respond to him.

Trent Tanner, for pity's sake. What was it about the full-grown, virile version of Trent that brought out the hibernating wild streak in her? A streak that—for obvious reasons—she'd kept under control her whole life. Even though her parents had never pushed her into a mold, she'd always felt that as the local preacher's daughter, she'd had a duty—to behave herself, to set an example. To exhibit a modicum of decency and re-spect. To keep her baser instincts at bay.

Why, then, after years of a virtuous life-style, could Trent reduce her to a wanton hussy in the twinkling of a sky-blue eye?

"Oh," she groaned miserably. She'd made a first-class fool of herself, responding to him with such carefree abandon.

She didn't have time to waste on a man like Trent. No. She had a game plan. She knew her prayers for a dark-haired man with a mustache and twinkling green eyes would be answered. MaryJane and John's father would make his appearance soon enough, and when he did, he would protect her from the likes of men such as Trent Tanner.

Funny, though—she mused as she listened to the rain beat a furious tattoo on her roof—how he'd landed on her bed that way in the middle of her prayer for a husband.

Could he be the one? she wondered, entertaining the ludi-crous idea for a brief moment. The Lord worked in mysterious ways, she knew, but in her opinion, this was downright scary. She couldn't even begin to imagine marriage and children with the boy who'd routinely tempted her to break the commandment regarding murder.

Rolling over, she scrunched her pillow into a tortured lump and vowed that she wouldn't give Trent another thought. She needed her beauty rest. The rain cloud overhead passed, and it was suddenly silent in her bedroom. Opening her eyes, she peered through the darkness toward the wall that connected to the Skinners' apartment and listened. Just exactly what she was listening for, she couldn't say. What did swindlers sound like? Stuffing a mattress with money probably didn't make much noise.

Disgusted with herself for letting her imagination become nearly as overactive as Trent's, she flopped over and stared out her window.

Were the Skinners really conning innocent people? Gracious. She nervously twisted the satin binding on her blanket. Rupert was such a sweetie. So were his three best friends down at the retirement center.

Clementine was a bossy, gruff, opinionated older woman with a heart as big as all outdoors. The well-padded woman enjoyed many indulgences forbidden by her doctor, most notably her chewing tobacco. This she tried to sneak past Prudence on a regular basis, but the indelicate bulge in her lower lip was hard to miss.

Then there was Norvil, a slight man who favored cardigan sweaters and complaining. But, however crotchety Norvil liked to appear, underneath all the bluster, he was a softie.

Hetta was a tiny birdlike creature who still, at well over eighty, wore false eyelashes. And false teeth. And false hair. And—well, Prudence was only guessing here—falsies. As the resident siren, Hetta believed in keeping up appearances. She was forgetful, but sweet-tempered, and generous to a fault.

Sitting bolt upright in bed, Prudence gathered the hem of

her blanket into a frustrated bunch and clutched it under her chin.

What if it was true? What if Trent was right? She couldn't stand to think of any of her little dearies being hurt. Like Trent, she felt an incredible urge to protect these people who had become family to her.

Her eyes narrowed in the darkness. She had to admit, when it came to the Skinners, they really were quite mysterious. They'd just shown up in Howatowa out of the blue. No family, no job to lure them to town.

Unless of course, she counted Fantasy Investments. Taking a deep breath, Prudence exhaled, trying to blow her confusion away. Dropping back on her bed, she buried her face in her pillow and screamed with frustration, the way she used to at least once a week until the Tanner family moved to Seattle.

This whole thing was driving her crazy.

"Fantasy Investments," she muttered into the night. "What the heck kind of a name is that?"

After a restless night spent on a lumpy bed at the old Howatowa Hotel, Trent dragged himself to an upright position and winced. Man, he was sore. And here he'd been under the impression that he was in pretty good shape. It would seem that climbing around in a cramped attic late at night required muscle groups he hadn't even known existed. Then again, falling through the ceiling might have something to do with the terminal case of stiffness from which he was suffering this morning. Gingerly, he hoisted himself out of bed and, rubbing his aching back as he went, limped over to the antique washbasin.

In its heyday, the Howatowa Hotel had been the little town's crown jewel. But now, like the rest of the community, it was gradually deteriorating.

He peered into the chipped mirror that hung askew on the faded red velvet wallpaper and thoughtfully rubbed the days' growth that shadowed his chin. The storm had passed and it was bright and clear this Monday morning. There was no place more beautiful than the coastal town of Howatowa, after a summer storm, he mused, beginning to realize just how much he'd missed his boyhood stomping grounds.

Grabbing his shaving kit, he fished out his toothbrush and loaded it with toothpaste. He knew he'd better get a move on. He had a lot to do today.

Aside from visiting his Uncle Rupert down at the retirement center, Trent wanted to make some subtle inquiries around town about Fantasy Investments. He also planned to make a few phone calls to some government agencies and bureaus to find out if there was any dirt regarding this suspicious company and their dealings in other parts of the country.

Then, when he was done with that, he had to go fix the hole in Prudence's ceiling.

He smiled wryly at his reflection and began to brush his teeth. She hadn't been too pleased with him last night. Just like the good old days.

Only now, he didn't want to goad her into a fury.

No. Now, he wanted to gain her attention in other ways. Ways that would make her forget the hoodlum he'd been back in grade school. Ways that would convince her that he was right about this Skinner scam. The way it stood now, if he was going to pull this thing off and bring the Skinners to justice, he had to have her help. Rinsing his mouth, he popped his toothbrush in the hotel water glass, and leaned against the sink.

Like it or not, she was involved up to her beautiful green eyes in this whole mess. And, after last night, she didn't have much choice but to play along. Whether she wanted to admit it or not, he knew she was starting to think that maybe he was on to something with this phony resort deal.

Yeah, he thought as he grabbed a hand towel and wiped his mouth, she would help. She wouldn't want to, but she would help. She loved those senior citizens too much not to.

A slow smile spread across his face. Trent just couldn't believe his good fortune. After all these years, Prudence was still single. How could that be? Surely, someone as beautiful and loving as Prudence Mackelroy should be married by now and have a passel of youngsters tugging on her skirts.

For his part, he wondered if his boyhood fixation on her was one of the reasons he'd never taken the plunge himself. Not on a conscious level, perhaps. But looking back, no one he'd ever dated seemed to compare to his glorious memories of the feisty gal with the midnight curls.

Although, Lord knew, he'd given up hope that Prudence could ever care for him. Too many times he'd pushed the envelope just a little too far with her. Years ago he'd come to the realization that when it came to Prudence Mackelroy, he would have to settle for unrequited love.

And, until last night, he had.

But something had happened when he'd kissed her. Yep, Trent thought as he stared, unseeing, into the cracked and smoky mirror. Last night, just before he'd headed out into the storm—when he'd pulled her close and fulfilled his boyhood fantasy of kissing the preacher's daughter—Prudence Mackelroy had kissed him back.

With fire.

Passion.

The kind of ardent response he'd only dreamed of as a schoolboy.

Trent shook his head. The strangest part of it was, out of all the people in Howatowa that he could have dropped in on, he'd managed to fall through Prudence's ceiling and land on her bed. Talk about fate.

Well, if for some divine reason he was being given another chance with her, he sure as heck wasn't going to blow it. Not this time. Pushing himself away from the sink, he yanked some fresh clothes out of his suitcase and trotted toward the shower with a song on his lips. Suddenly, visiting the rather sterile, antiseptic-smelling Howatowa Retirement Center had taken on a new luster. He hadn't bothered much about his appearance the last two times he'd been there to visit Uncle Rupert. After all—crime busting aside—he was on vacation.

Although, he grinned to himself, the fact that he hadn't bothered to shave or get a recent haircut didn't seem to make much difference to the flirtatious Hetta. The way the sweet older woman carried on, batting those monstrous eyelashes at him and giggling so girlishly, one would think he was some kind of visiting dignitary.

Prudence, on the other hand, would be harder to impress. Perhaps he would slap on some of that new after-shave he'd gotten for his birthday. And, maybe he would wear his new black sweater. He was going to need all the weapons he could gather to convince her that he was respectable.

Whether she liked it or not, he needed her help.

It was social hour at the Howatowa Retirement Center. Of course, due to the low population of ambulatory residents, the untrained eye would not be able to tell the difference between the official social hour and any other hour. The recreation lounge was largely empty, with the exception of Rupert and three of his closest friends—Hetta, Norvil and Clementine. The four had gathered on folding chairs around an old metal table with a plastic top.

After spending some time quizzing Prudence about her cruise—and speculating about their own chances of going next summer—they finally settled into their daily habit of playing poker for bottle caps, and trading insults.

They were by far the liveliest of the two-dozen-or-so residents that composed the population of the retirement center, and as such, were the folks that had wormed their way permanently into Prudence's heart.

This being Monday morning, Prudence had some paperwork that needed doing before the new director arrived. Settling on the hard leather couch, with a cup of coffee and some charts and files, she leaned back in the warm patch of sunshine that streamed through the window. Out of the corner of her eye, she could loosely monitor the little group across the institutional-green room.

Trent's Uncle Rupert was acting as dealer, and as always, looked jaunty in his black visor and matching armband. Well into his eighth decade, Rupert had an uncommon zest for life. With great fanfare, he enthusiastically shuffled the deck, then tossed the cards furiously around the table.

"Come on, you old geezers," he roared gleefully, "ante up!" The chinking of bottle caps reverberated throughout the room as everyone reluctantly tossed their share into the middle of the table.

Leaning very slowly back in her seat at the table, Hetta peeked from under her spiky lashes and waved a gnarled finger at Prudence.

"Yoo-hoo, honey," she twittered, her quavery, operatic-like falsetto echoing across the linoleum. "When is that new director of ours going to get here?"

Prudence looked up from her file and smiled. "We're expecting him to arrive in town sometime tomorrow. I imagine he'll be by to meet us within a day or two."

"Come on, Hetta, old girl," Rupert thundered into her good ear. "It's your turn." When she didn't respond, Rupert turned her wrist so that he could see her hand.

Hetta ignored him. "Wha'd ya say his name was again, sugar?" she asked Prudence.

"Fresh Meat," Norvil muttered, then cackled with Rupert.

Prudence nibbled the end of her pencil and checked her file. "Uh, I've never met him. Let's see, his first name is Leonard. Leonard Frederick."

"Hmm." Hetta pursed her bright orange lips. "Is he single, honey?"

"I believe so."

Preening excitedly over this bit of news, Hetta tugged on her deep red sweater, arranging it to better display her rather prominent assets—the assets that seemed to change in size and stature according to Hetta's mood. "Do you know what he looks like, sugar?"

"What the hell difference does it make what he looks like?" Clementine barked crabbily in the gravelly baritone that had taken years of smoking to fine-tune. "Hit me," she rasped at Rupert.

"I'll hit you," Hetta snapped and fussed with her blue-gray wig.

"I'll bet you're hopin' the new guy will look like that big blond Apollo-type nephew of Rupert's," the curmudgeonly Norvil accused. "You'd like that, wouldn't ya, Hetta," he shouted. "The way you were drooling over poor old Trent, like some kind of…of—" Norvil groped for an adequate insult "—love-struck drooler, there."

Behind his cranky expression, there was a teasing glint in Norvil's eye. The routine for the little group was the same every day. They would shout and trade abuse all the livelong day, then come back the next for more of the same.

Wriggling with indignation, Hetta bristled. "I did not drool." She glowered at Norvil and tossed some bottle caps into the ante pile with a shaky hand. "Rupert," she queried, slowly turning toward him, "speaking of your nephew Trent, when is he coming back for a visit?"

Prudence hated herself for the way she leaned forward to catch Rupert's reply.

"Any minute now, toots," he said, blatantly pulling a card from the bottom of the deck and stuffing it into his shirt pocket for later use. "Said he'd be over this morning to say howdy before he heads out to take care of some business."

Prudence's heart jolted into her throat, making it difficult to breathe. Trent was coming over here? This morning? Her face burst into flame as once again she recalled how enthusiastically she'd returned his kiss last night. For heaven's sake. She still couldn't figure out what had gotten into her. Trent most likely thought she was some kind of sex-crazed lunatic. First she yelled at him and called him names, then she grabbed hold of the back of his head and kissed him as if there was no tomorrow.

"What kind of business?" Hetta asked, her voice throbbing breathlessly.

"Didn't say," Rupert replied with a shrug.

Yikes, Prudence thought, jumping to her feet. Maybe she should run along and hide in her office. She just couldn't face Trent. It was too soon. It was too mortifying. It was too easy to forget that she already had a man out there—somewhere. A solid, dependable man who resembled her sweet papa.

Not a man with silky blond hair and eyes so blue you could swim in them. Not an irreverent thrill seeker who spent his off hours spying on nice little old folks like the Skinners. In the calm, rational light of day, she'd decided that Trent must be mistaken about her neighbors.

Clutching her coffee cup in one hand and her files in the other, Prudence made her way across the lounge and toward her office. Her progress was halted, however, by something Clementine was saying.

"Did Harry Skinner tell you how much you owe on that mansion you won yet, Rupert?" the woman queried, her gravelly voice causing Prudence's head to snap around.

Rupert rubbed his callused hands together and cackled gleefully. "Not yet. Soon, though. It won't be much, I'm sure. Just a few thousand bucks, more or less, and the place is mine."

Prudence stared in shock at the trusting Rupert. A few thousand bucks, more or less? Clamping her gaping jaw shut, she wondered, was this what Trent was talking about? Her gaze darted worriedly around the small group at the table and finally landed on Trent who had just arrived and was watching her from the doorway across the room.

Seeing him standing there, leaning against the doorframe, his arms crossed casually over his broad chest, the sun glinting off his shiny golden head, had an odd effect on her. He exuded strength. A new maturity. He cared about these people. He could take care of them. In some ways she was greatly relieved that he was there.

In others, she was greatly disturbed. How could a single glimpse of those sexy blue eyes across a room have her stomach roiling and her heart all atwitter this way? She would have to be extremely careful around him, she thought, disgusted at this weakness she seemed to have suddenly developed where he was concerned.

His brows were raised, and he inclined his head at the excitedly chattering table. The look in his eyes said "See what I mean?" as clearly as if he'd spoken the words aloud.

She nodded imperceptibly. She could see.

"Well, Rupert, you lucky old dog, that calls for a celebration," Clementine said with a grunt. Reaching into her massive purse, she withdrew several bags of candy and dumped them on the table. "When my ship comes in from this resort deal, I'm gonna buy me a boat. I always wanted to learn to water-ski," she added quite seriously.

Prudence and Trent exchanged perplexed glances over their heads.

"Hit me," Norvil commanded Rupert. "Yep." His lower lip protruded thoughtfully as he stroked his boney chin. "If this resort the Skinners are talking about takes off—and it sounds like it should—we'll all be rollin' in dough." He lifted a brow at Hetta. "How about you, tootsie? How are you going to spend your fortune?"

Hetta shrugged. "I don't know. There are so many things I still want to do. Most likely, though, I'll go with bust-enhancement surgery."

Suffering a sudden coughing attack, Trent inadvertently announced his presence.

"Trent!" Hetta trilled and pulled her shoulders back as far as her arthritis would allow. "Dearie, you're here! Come give us a little smooch," she demanded, puckering her lips into a giant orange bunch.

"How are my two best girls?" he asked, grinning mischievously as he crossed the room and pecked the two older woman lightly on the forehead.

Clementine scowled. "You're so full of it. We know we're not your favorite," she blustered, loving the attention.

"Busted," Trent agreed affably, patting Clementine's arm. "You must have heard the news, then."

"What news?" Hetta loved news.

"That I've finally gotten back together with the true love of my life after all these years." He lifted a meaningful eyebrow at Prudence whose eyes suddenly widened in fear.

"Say what?" Rupert grinned broadly, revealing the fact that he'd neglected to put all this teeth in this morning. "Who's the lucky girl?"

"Why," Trent said, walking over to where Prudence stood and looped a casual arm around her shoulders, "Prudie, here, of course. I thought by now she would have told you all that we were an item again."

"No kidding?" Rupert swung his happy gaze to Prudence.

"Uh…" Prudence stared dully at the older man, her mouth still agape. "Now wait just a minute—"

"Oh, sweetheart, let's not wait another minute!" Trent dropped a possessive kiss on her forehead. "I guess she didn't tell you yet because she…wants to keep me all to herself." Reaching out, he tugged a lock of her hair and tossed an indulgent smile down at her red face before shifting his impish gaze to the four at the table.

"No…" Prudence's eyes darted wildly around the table. "No, I, that's not… I, uh…"

"She's always saying how she wants to keep our special love a private affair. But that's so hard for me. I just want to shout it from the rafters."

"Trent!" When Prudence finally found her voice it was filled with indignation. "That's not true and you know it, you big—"

He planted a quick kiss on her still-protesting lips, then, clapping a playful hand over her mouth, he grinned down at her. "Darling, don't be afraid to let the world know. They would find out sooner or later. We can't keep our unique love a secret anymore. Sweetheart, don't worry about…sullying my reputation."

"Sullying *your* reputation?" she sputtered.

"She hates it when I reduce our special feelings toward each other into mere words, don't you, my little rapscallion?"

Prudence blushed so furiously, even the palms of her hands went pink.

Nudging his uncle on the shoulder, Trent grinned down at him. "No offense, Uncle Rupert, but you can't have thought I'd spend the entire summer in Howatowa just visiting you. Not when there was such a beautiful woman waiting here for me, after all these years." He darted a loving glance down at Prudence.

"Waiting for *you?*" She gripped a handful of his black sweater in her fists. "Trent! I demand that you tell these people the truth!"

"Yes, it's true," he nodded in solemn agreement. "A beautiful woman that I've loved ever since I was in short pants." He cleared his throat. That part was true enough. "Luckily, fate saw fit to throw us back together during my stay in Howatowa."

"Well, I'll be a monkey's uncle," Rupert cried, pounding joyfully on the table and sending bottle caps flying.

"Yes," Prudence agreed in a tightly controlled voice. "That would be true."

"Now, now, sweetheart," Trent admonished lightly and gripped her elbow with the same warning he'd imparted last night in front of the Skinners. "I see no reason not to let these good people in on our secret. I think it's the only solution. All things considered." His eyes stabbed into hers.

Grabbing a folding chair of his own, he lowered his lanky frame between Hetta and Clementine and pulled the astonished Prudence into his lap, where he held her captive in his ironclad embrace.

She struggled to put some space between her body and his, but finally conceded the fact that Clementine would most likely learn to water-ski before she could wangle her way out of Trent's steely grasp. Closing her eyes, Prudence dropped her head into her hands and rubbed her throbbing temples.

"Oh, yes." Trent smiled grandly and proceeded to regale them with the romantic tale. "We were really something in the ninth grade, weren't we, Prudie-pie?"

"We were something, all right," Prudence huffed, refusing to look at him. Finally, she pasted a brittle smile on her face for the benefit of her audience and leaned toward him. "I don't believe I agreed to help you in this counterintelligence spy game of yours," she hissed into his ear.

Trent cheerfully ignored her lack of enthusiasm. "Oh, it's true. Back then she could barely keep her hands off me, but I played it cool. Right, hon?"

"Oh, *please*," Prudence muttered so only he could hear. "When I get done with you, you'll wish I'd kept my hands off you, all right..." Her arctic smile could have freeze-dried the coffee in Hetta's cup.

Laughing, Trent pried her fingers out of their rather tenacious grip on his neck and nuzzled her cheek with his nose. "I'm just so glad we found each other after all this time."

"Here, here," Clementine rasped. Reaching into her purse, she extracted a tin of chewing tobacco and offered it up to Trent. "Care for a dip?"

"No thanks, Clementine. Prudence won't kiss me."

"Party pooper," the older woman muttered, stuffing the tin back into the bag with the rest of her contraband. "Then I guess you won't want a cigar, either." She sighed and shook her head.

Rupert reached across Hetta and thumped Trent soundly on the back. "Why, I had no idea you two were so close back in school," he crowed. "What a happy surprise that you found each other again."

Trent nodded and tightened his grip on Prudence's slender

waist. "I know. It came as a bit of a surprise to me too. Falling for her—" his eyes shimmered with an age-old mischief "—that way again, after so many years. It was almost as though I'd been struck by lightning."

"And—" Prudence gasped loudly as he dipped his tongue into the shell of her ear "—if God is in his heaven, you surely will be." Her voice sounded reedy and breathless.

Carefree laughter rang out from deep in Trent's chest. "Now, Prudie-pie," he cajoled. "Is that any way for you to talk to the man of your dreams? The veritable answer to your prayer, if I may be so bold?"

Eyes suddenly wide and flashing, Prudence twisted in his lap and searched his face.

Trent wondered what was going through her mind. Whatever it was, she looked as though she'd seen a ghost. Then as quickly as it had come, the look passed and she shook her head vehemently, as if to clear it of some unfortunate thought.

"Naw," she muttered.

Rupert could barely contain his joy. "This is just wonderful! Son," he roared at Trent, "your father would have been so proud."

Trent froze as a sudden pang of guilt assailed him. It went against his nature to lie to a group of sweet folks this way, but dammit, he had his reasons. It was for their own good. If they believed that he and Prudence were in love, then they couldn't blurt out the unfortunate truth to the Skinners. And, as long as the devious Skinners believed that he and Prudence were in love, he could continue to spy on them, undetected, from the safety of her bedroom.

Besides, he thought, trying to soothe his prickling conscience, he did have a thing for Prudence. The fact that it was a one-sided affair wasn't his fault.

"I think he would have, too," Trent agreed, planting another kiss on Prudence's nose. He knew she was fit to be tied, but he couldn't seem to help himself. She was just so darn kissable. Now that he had her exactly where he'd wanted her since they were in grade school together, he couldn't help but take advantage of the situation. She smelled so wonderful—fresh and clean. And he loved the way her hair tickled his cheek as he nibbled her earlobe.

"You're so lucky," Hetta sniffed at Prudence, rapidly blinking the tears of joy that threatened to ruin her makeup. Reaching into her brassiere, she extracted a giant handful of tissue and dabbed at her lashes.

Prudence attempted a smile. "Trent," she chirped perkily through her tightly clenched jaw, "I would appreciate it if you would please keep your lips on your own face."

"Oh, I'm sorry," he mumbled sheepishly. "It's just that I've missed you so much this morning. And after last night, well…" He let his sentence die, much to the dismay of their aged audience.

Prudence smiled weakly at the little group. "I'm gonna kill you," she muttered for his ears only.

"That sounds like fun." Trent cocked a devilish brow and shifted her to a more comfortable position on his lap. "Honey, the reason I stopped by, aside from visiting my uncle, was to let you know that I'll be over at your place again tonight." To the rest of the group he confided, "I have to help her clean up a mess we made in her bedroom last night."

"Trent!" Prudence shrieked.

"Yes, sweetheart. You don't have to yell, I'm right here."

"I mean it! Tell them the truth!"

"About what? The hole we made in the ceiling above your bed? Or would you rather I go into detail about the costumes?" His brow furrowed in a perplexed little rut.

"Tell them it's not what they think," she ordered, cuffing his ear in outrage.

"Oww." He pouted at her, then turned to face the four pairs of eyes that looked on with rapt attention. "It's not what you think," he parroted, sounding thoroughly unconvincing.

"Trent."

She had that murderous look in her eye again—the look that made him want to kiss her senseless.

"What?" Shrugging boyishly, he nudged Prudence off his lap with great reluctance. He would have liked to spend his whole day right there, doing nothing but holding her and kissing those delectable lips of hers. But, alas, he had pressing business.

He had a couple of felons to bring down. If he was lucky, he'd have a chance to steal another kiss tonight, if the Skinners were around. Until then, he would just have to spend the day dreaming about her.

"Listen, honey, I've got to be on my way. How about if I meet you back at your place after work?" The four sets of bespectacled eyes swung back and forth between the two. "I'll have all the tools I need for us to get to work in the bedroom. You fix us something to eat, okay?"

Prudence was too mortified to respond.

"You did change the sheets after I left last night? After the way we'd been jumping around..."

"Get out of here!" Prudence shrieked, and pointed at the door.

"Okay, babe. Later," Trent called jauntily over his shoulder as he disappeared into the sunshine.

Prudence turned to face the slack jawed and bug-eyed group. "It's not what you think," she explained woefully.

Dumbfounded, the four seniors simply nodded.

Chapter Five

Prudence had no idea why she was going to such elaborate measures to prepare a meal for Trent. Especially considering the bizarre scene he'd engineered for the benefit of Rupert and his friends that morning. She could still feel his arms tightly circling her waist as he explained their—her heart picked up speed—*special* love. What a crock.

Sighing, she pushed her hair away from her face. No, he didn't deserve such special treatment tonight. So, why was she pulling out the big cookbooks?

It couldn't be because he'd looked so impressive in that black sweater he'd worn, with the sleeves pushed up to the elbow. And it definitely wasn't because of that amazingly sexy after-shave that clung to her own skin, even now. No, she thought defensively as she added sprigs of mint to the glazed baby carrots, it wasn't as if she was trying to impress him or anything.

She'd simply been in the mood for new potatoes, homemade biscuits with real butter, and a Caesar salad with freshly grated Parmesan cheese. Her doorbell rang as she was basting the pot roast. It had to be Trent.

An unwelcome shiver of excitement danced down her spine. Pushing the oven door shut, she rushed to the bathroom to check her makeup. One glimpse of her sparkly eyes and flushed cheeks had her frowning at her absurd behavior. She was acting like a giddy schoolgirl, which was odd. Even as a giddy schoolgirl, Prudence had never acted like one. Shaking her finger sternly at her reflection she took a deep breath, donned a cool mask of nonchalance and stepped lightly to her foyer to answer her door.

"Hi, honey! I'm home," Trent bellowed for the benefit of her nefarious neighbors and with a roguish grin, swept her into his arms for a welcome-home kiss.

"Would you knock it off," Prudence hissed, wriggling out of his arms so that his lips missed their mark and ended up making a rather pleasant wet spot on her temple. She rubbed at it with her apron as she threw the door shut after him.

"Wow," he said appreciatively, as he shrugged out of his jacket and sniffed the succulent aromas that were emanating from her kitchen. "What smells so good?"

"Dinner," Prudence informed him, struggling to reapply her cool mask of nonchalance. Which wasn't easy, considering she was still more than a little embarrassed over having made such an idiot of herself right her on this very spot with him last night.

Rapscallion. Why had she called him that? She wasn't even sure she knew what it meant. And, sully. For crying out loud. She sounded like her grandmother. Trent had taken great delight in pointing that out in front of everyone this morning. Luckily, Rupert and the gang hadn't understood the references.

Tonight, she would show him that she was no longer that prissy, uptight girl he knew in school. Although, why this should be so important to her, was a puzzle. She'd never cared what Trent thought about her in the past. Well, she would figure that out later. For tonight, anyway, no matter how crazy he drove her, she would try to roll with the punches. She was an adult now. She would act like one.

"Man." Trent shook his hair out of his face. "Whatever you're cooking makes me wish I hadn't stopped at the Burger Box on the way over."

Prudence stared at him, agog. "You stopped at the *Burger Box?*" she cried, her shoulders sagging. So much for rolling with the punches. "But," she protested, "you told me to fix us... Oh—" she sighed resignedly "—never mind."

He lifted and dropped his hands. "Yeah, but the way you were scowling at me, I didn't think you'd cook anything. It sure smells killer in there," he said, sending a longing look over her shoulder into the kitchen. "Did you go to all that trouble just for me?" He seemed inordinately pleased by her gesture.

"It's no big deal," she chirped, waving an airy hand toward her afternoon's labors as they simmered on the stove. "I always make myself a...well-rounded meal." She guessed TV dinners were well-rounded. Prudence could tell by the look on his face that he didn't believe a word of it and she was more embarrassed now than ever. Turning to hide the flames in her cheeks, she moved back into her tiny kitchen and grabbed her rolling pin.

"Wow. I usually just have cereal for dinner," he said over his shoulder, admiration tingeing his voice. "Sometimes, when I'm feeling really culinary, I'll fix toast, too. Listen Prude," he continued hopefully as he tossed his jacket over the back of her sofa. "Since it's still really early in the evening, save me a plate and I'll eat as soon as I've done a few things to your bedroom ceiling. That'll give me a chance to work up another appetite," he said, as he ambled into the kitchen.

Prudence slammed a pile of piecrust dough down on the countertop. "Whatever," she said blithely, hoping her mortification wasn't too obvious.

What a fool. She should have known better than to have gone to all that trouble for Trent Tanner, she thought as she pounded the dough with her fists. He must think she was some kind of sorry old spinster, the way she'd kissed him last night, then cooked for him tonight. He probably thought she was trying to trap him in her pathetic web.

If she'd been smart, she would have told him she had a date tonight. Trouble was, she didn't. In her line of work, it was tough to meet a decent single man under the age of sixty-five. She doubted Trent would have felt too threatened if she'd announced she would be having dinner and taking in a show with Norvil.

With arched brows, Trent watched her wield her rolling pin. "I'll unload the tools I rented from my car in a minute, but first I thought you'd be interested in what I found out about the Skinners today."

Pulling one of her wooden chairs away from her table, he turned it around, stuffed it between his legs and, dropping into it, slung his elbows over the back.

As she lifted the rolling pin off the piecrust she'd been energetically rolling, Prudence's eyes darted to his. "You found something out?"

A satisfied look crossed his face. "I'm off to a good start, at any rate." His gaze dropped to the rolling pin she held between her hands. "But first, you have to promise not to use that on me, okay?" he teased.

Glancing down, she smiled ruefully, then went back to work. "Don't give me any ideas," she warned. "So, what did you find out?" She tried to sound cool. Blasé. Disinterested, even.

Prudence didn't want Trent thinking that she'd already agreed to participate in his harebrained scheme, even though she suspected she was already involved more than she cared to admit. However, it would take some pretty serious convincing on his part for her to let him do something as devious as using her place to spy on her neighbors.

Trent pulled a small notebook out of his hip pocket and flipped through several pages. "Well, first, I called the Better Business Bureau."

"And?"

"Never heard of 'em."

Her eyes widened. "Really?" Prudence tightly gripped the handles of the rolling pin, suddenly feeling anything but disinterested. "Wow."

"Yeah, wow." Trent nodded and slapped his notebook against his palm. "Then I called the attorney general's office and told them about Rupert winning the mansion in the raffle and the sketchy resort plans and the whole ball of wax."

"What did they say?"

"Well, they wanted to look a few things up, but the general consensus was there was probably some ordinance or statute that they'd infracted with their activities. Lotteries like that are tricky. You have to go through a whole lot of red tape to set it up legally and everything." He rubbed his chin. "They're going to call me back with more information later, since I was speaking to a clerical staff member who didn't have all the answers I needed. But, she was inclined to think that the Skinners might have broken a few laws."

"No kidding," Prudence breathed, pushing the forgotten piecrust out of the way and leaning against the counter toward him. Burning nervous energy, she spun the rolling pin loosely in her hands.

"Yeah." Trent's face lit as he warmed to his subject. His words began to tumble out in an excited jumble, and he waved his hands to emphasize certain points. "Then I called the State Real Estate Commission. Whenever great amounts of land trade hands on a deal like this," he explained for her benefit, "they can check on the licenses of the parties involved and the like. Anyway, these people sounded worried, too, and said they're going to check a few things out and get back to me."

"Man." Prudence's eyes were wide with wonder. "You were busy."

Trent scooted his chair forward so that he could reach the Caesar salad. Snagging a crouton, he said, "Yeah, well, wait till you hear this!'' Suddenly, he sniffed the air. "Is something burning?"

"Oh!" As Prudence whirled around, the rolling pin in her hand caught the sheet of freshly baked biscuits and sent it sailing to the floor. "Oh, shoot!" she cried in dismay as she yanked the newly scorched new potatoes and the badly singed baby carrots off the stove top and onto her breadboard.

Springing out of his chair, Trent dropped to his knees and chased after the runaway biscuits. "Here you go," he said, blowing on the biscuits that hadn't fallen apart and brushing them off on his sweater. "Good as new." Rising to his feet, he set his booty on the counter.

Prudence sighed heavily, and swept his helpful pile into the dustbin. "You can't eat them after they've rolled around on the floor," she chided.

Openmouthed, Trent stared yearningly into her garbage pail at the biscuits. "Why not?" he asked, genuinely puzzled.

"Oh, Trent, really." Turning off the burners and tossing a dish towel over the acrid-smelling scorched pots, she took a resigned breath and looked expectantly at Trent. "Never mind." She exhaled and waved him back into his chair. "Go on with your story. Please."

Tiny lines formed at the corners of Trent's eyes, as he settled back into his chair and went on enthusiastically with his story.

"Okay, uh... I called the Washington State Financial Fraud Section, and spoke with an investigator named Mart. He's going to try to get me a printout of all the complaints that may have been filed against Fantasy Investments. If he can find them, that is. There was nothing on them in his computer. Anyway, Mart thinks the Fantasy Investments company is as phony as a three-dollar bill." Trent sat back and shot her a smug smile.

"No kidding! Really?" Prudence pounded the countertop in amazement, causing her aluminum salad bowl to teeter off the edge. Dumbfounded, both she and Trent watched as it fell to the floor, bounced several times, spun in a few crazy circles and finally came to a rest at her feet. "Clearly—" she sighed, bending to the floor and scooping the greens back into the bowl "—this meal was not meant to be."

"Oh, come on, Prudie. A little dirt never killed anybody." Joining her on the floor, Trent crawled around gathering bits of lettuce and blowing on them. "Now don't go and throw this away," he said, wiping a leaf on his pants and tossing it into her bowl. "Just wash it off. If you don't, there isn't going to be anything left to eat."

"You already ate," she drawled, looking dubiously into the bedraggled salad bowl.

"Yeah, but I'm a growing boy." He smiled winsomely at her as he clasped her hands in his and assisted her to her feet.

"So I noticed," she blurted out, her eyes darting over his impressive physique before she could stop herself. She felt a blush crawl up her neck and land in her cheeks.

Darn. She hated when she gave in to prurient impulses like that. What was it about Trent that always made her feel off-kilter?

"Anyway," she continued blithely, deciding to ignore his lopsided grin, "Mart thinks the Skinners' company is phony, huh?"

"He says it sure looks that way to him. For starters, when he couldn't find any history on them or their so-called company in the computer, he started asking me about the mansion Rupert won. The way they're handling that particular transaction looks suspicious to him, especially since they seem to be targeting only senior citizens with all of their marketing." Trent looked up from his notes. "I did some checking around town today. It seems that no one under the age of sixty-five has ever heard of Fantasy Investments."

"Well, I'll be..." Prudence murmured, fascinated.

His gaze swept back over the notes he'd taken from his conversation with Mart. "Oh, yeah, and the fact that the Skinners are older themselves strikes Mart as a little odd. He says he's seen this kind of thing before. You know, an unscrupulous company preying on senior citizens this way." Trent sighed and looked her straight in the eye. "It's almost always bad news."

Prudence moved over and sank into one of her kitchen chairs. "How horrible," she murmured, looking worriedly at him. "What are we going to do?" For the first time in her life, she had a feeling that Trent wasn't leading her down the garden path. This was no grade-school science project. This was serious business.

"We?" Trent arched a curious brow. "You're willing to help?"

Resting her elbows on the table, she laced her fingers together and rested her chin on the backs of her knuckles. "I guess I don't have much choice, do I? First of all, by now I'm sure half the town thinks we are already living in sin." With a heartfelt sigh, she shook her head and closed her eyes. "So, I guess I don't have much to lose in the reputation department anymore. Secondly, if everything you tell me is true—and I have no reason to believe you'd lie about this, Trent..." She looked at him with raised brows.

"Of course not," he answered her seriously. His handsome face reflected an earnest desire to help his uncle.

She nodded, believing him. "In that case, I can't stand the idea of my friends losing their money to these crooks any more than you can. It would be crazy not to help you."

"So you'll help?"

Prudence took a deep breath. "I'll help."

"Great!" Trent whooped loudly at the ceiling and waved his fists in triumph. "Wonderful!" he cried, and grinned broadly at her. "You won't regret this, Prudie, I swear."

Why did she suddenly feel the same sense of foreboding that she'd felt when Trent had picked her as his biology-lab partner back in the ninth grade? "I'd better not." Grabbing the rolling pin, she pointed it threateningly at him. "Don't make me use this."

"Don't worry, I'm not into anything kinky." His grin was sexy as he wiggled his brows up and down at her.

"That's not what you told Mr. Skinner," she retorted with a grin. Prudence sighed and shook her head. "What have I gotten myself into?" She sent this question heavenward, then looked seriously at Trent. "Where do we start, and what do you want me to do?"

Resting his arms on the back of the chair, Trent regarded her thoughtfully. "Well, just letting me check on the Skinners from your place is a big help. It sure beats crawling into your attic from the vent under the eaves." He grinned. "I'm not getting any younger."

"Okay. No problem. Anything else?" Prudence looked expectantly at him.

"As long as the Skinners think we're a couple, they won't be suspicious about my being here. That's why I told Uncle Rupert and his friends that we were an item today. If they all believe that we're in love, then they can't tip the Skinners off." He slanted a curious glance at her. "Think you can pull it off?"

"Pull what off?"

"Pretending to...you know. Love me."

Prudence felt yet another wave of heat crawl up her neck and wash over her cheeks. Squirming in her seat she said, "I can act."

"Good." Trent dropped his chin onto his arm and looked at her from beneath the lazy hoods of his eyes. "I think it'll be fun."

As their eyes met, she felt her heart pick up speed. "Just don't get too carried away," she said, bristling.

"I won't. Besides," he reasoned, his low voice causing gooseflesh to dance riotously down her arms and legs, "it won't be forever."

"I know," Prudence managed in a squeaky voice. She cleared her throat and went on. "It just seems wrong to lie to them that way."

"I'm sorry, Prudie." Trent looked sympathetic. "But, it's for their own good. They won't hold this little white lie against us, once they see the Skinners revealed for what they really are."

She nodded slightly. This really went against the grain for her, but she knew Trent had a point. If the folks at the retirement center didn't believe that she and Trent were dating, there was no telling what might get back to the Skinners. It wouldn't do to have the Skinners get suspicious of them. Not at this stage of the game. "Anything else?"

"Yes." Trent leaned forward, warming to his subject. "You can keep your ear to the ground down at the retirement center. And get back to me with what you hear about the Skinners' plans every night after you get home from work."

His eyes were positively glowing as he sat up excitedly in his chair, his mind racing with plans to save his uncle from disaster. Prudence had to admire this about him. How many men would give up their summer vacation, and go to such lengths, just to bail a gullible relative out of trouble? Not many, she was sure.

"And another thing," he continued, "we need to get to know the Skinners on a neighborly basis. Then maybe we can get them to tell us what they're up to."

"One thing at a time," Prudence cautioned. "Don't get too carried away all at once. Right now, you should probably get to work on my ceiling. Maybe you can overhear something incriminating from next door."

"Check. I'll go get the tools out of my trunk." Trent levered himself out of his chair, and swung with that easy gait of his out into her living room. Snagging his jacket off the back of her sofa, he sniffed the air. "Prudence?" he called over his shoulder.

"Hmm?"

"Is something burning again?"

He grinned at her sharp intake of breath and watched with interest as she whirled and whipped open her oven door.

"Oh, phooey," she moaned as she rescued what was a rather dark and steamy-looking pile of meat from her oven, and fanned dispiritedly at it with her pot holder. "So much for dinner," she muttered, and tossed her baking pan into her sink where it landed with a hiss.

"I can always run back to the Burger Box, honey," Trent offered, a slow grin splitting his face.

"Honey," Prudence warned, "if you know what's good for you, you'll crawl up in the attic where you belong." Picking up the rolling pin, she shook it at him. "And stay there."

For half an hour now, Trent had lain—in a most horrendously cramped and bent position—in the attic over the Skinners' apartment, listening to their mundane conversation. He was beginning to think that they were on to him.

That had to be it. They must know he was listening and were speaking in some kind of gangster code. Could they have heard him thumping around up here and gotten suspicious? That was the only explanation Trent could come up with for their deliberately boring exchange.

As far as he could tell, they were in their kitchen. Baking cookies. For an orphanage, no less. Ha. Did they think he was born yesterday? There was no orphanage in Howatowa.

Yeah. They knew he was listening. They were being so obvious. Eventually they would let their guard down, and when they did, he would be there to gather the incriminating evidence. He attempted to shift his long body into a more comfortable position, but only succeeded in banging his head on the Skinners' rafters.

"What was that?" Mrs. Skinner asked anxiously.

"What?" This from Mr. Skinner.

"That noise."

"I don't know. Probably…" Mr. Skinner mumbled something that had the missus laughing.

Something that sounded vaguely like "Rabbits in the attic." Or "mad bats." Man. Trent glanced around uneasily. He sure

as hell hoped that wasn't true. Leaning forward, he strained
to hear, and in the process, smashed his elbow on their floor
joist. He grimaced. Damn. If they didn't know he was eavesdropping before, they sure did now.

"There it is again," Mrs. Skinner exclaimed.

"I'll get up there later and make sure no one is *hanging*
around," Mr. Skinner promised in a low voice.

"Good idea. Oh, Harry," Mrs. Skinner called to her husband. "I think we're out of sugar. I need at least..."

It was silent for a moment, and Trent pressed his ear more
firmly to the attic floor.

"Two cups." Another silence. Then she continued in a
lower voice. "Do you think you should go next door?"

"Now?" Harry Skinner asked. There was another silence
and then some laughter. "Gladys, you are bad." More laughter. More murmured conversation that Trent couldn't make
out.

"Shh," one of them cautioned in a whisper. More silence.

"Yeah." This from Harry. "I think you're right. It would
be good to go over there. And this is the perfect excuse.
But...what if...?"

"Wait," Gladys Skinner called. "I'll go with you. We'll
take the dog."

"Good idea."

Uh-oh. Trent winced in pain. His foot had fallen asleep.
And, they were coming. Wriggling as fast as he could to the
opening over Prudence's bed, he jumped onto her mattress.
He would have to buy her a new comforter. This one was
shot. Rolling to the floor, he limped through her living room
dragging his numb foot behind him and made it to the front
door, just as the bell rang.

"Hello, hello," he said grandly, welcoming the shady pair
inside. Sheesh. It felt like he'd broken his ankle. Pins and
needles shot through his leg as his foot began to wake up.

"Hello," Mrs. Skinner returned, following her husband into
the living room. She clutched a measuring cup to her chest.

She was good, Trent thought, watching the dog stagger after them, tripping over his floor-length ears as he went. She was going to play the part of sweet little granny to the hilt. Well, fine with him, he thought, shifting his narrow gaze from the dog to the couple. He didn't buy it for a minute.

Criminy. They didn't even look like they'd been baking. There was no flour on their clothes or anything. Heck, the few times he'd made cookies, he looked as if he'd been in a war.

"We were wondering if you could spare a cup or two of sugar," Mrs. Skinner asked sweetly, and held her cup out to Trent.

"Sure," Trent said, herding them over to the sofa. "Make yourselves at home, while I check with the…uh, little woman." He bestowed them with what he hoped was his most charming, trusting smile.

"Hey, babe," he called into the kitchen, where Prudence stood at the sink humming along with the radio and scrubbing a scorched pot. "Have you got a little sugar for me?" He tossed the double entendre out for the Skinners' benefit.

"Trent." Prudence sighed in exasperation, and snapped off the radio. Drying her hands on her apron, she strode out to the living room. "I don't know what you think you're trying to prove, but I'd appreciate it if you'd keep the sugar thing to a dull— Oh, hello," she chirped, noticing the Skinners. She shot a questioning look at Trent and pasted a wide smile on her face. "Honey? I didn't know we had company…."

"Yes, sweetheart. Isn't it wonderful? The Skinners are here! And, they brought their doggy."

Prudence's gaze dropped to the dog as it wobbled over to the sofa and with much distressful heaving, proceeded to lose its lunch at Mr. Skinner's feet.

"So I see."

"Oh, merciful heavens," Mrs. Skinner cried, and laughed a mortified laugh. "I'm so sorry. Willard hasn't been feeling well all day."

"That's okay. Trent, you won't mind tidying that up, will

you, honey?'' Prudence asked sweetly. "The paper towels are in the kitchen.''

"Oh. Uh. Sure.'' He could tell that Prudence was enjoying herself. Paying him back for falling through her ceiling, no doubt. Probably for the skunk and the poison oak, too. Oh, well, he thought with a grin as he tore off about ten feet of paper towel, he deserved it.

Prudence made idle chitchat with the Skinners while Trent held his breath and cleaned up after Willard. The dog watched him through sagging, bloodshot eyes—eyes that missed nothing. Trent had the feeling that the rotten mutt had spewed on purpose.

Once he'd dispensed with the odious task, Trent smiled at the Skinners and leaped to his feet. "Sugar, huh?'' he asked jovially. Clapping his hands together, he turned and looked at Prudence. "We keep our sugar in the kitchen, right, honey? Why don't you go get it out, and I'll help. I'll just, uh, carry the cup, uh—'' he bounded over and snatched the cup out of Mrs. Skinner's hands ''—here.''

Before Prudence could protest that she didn't need his help, he ushered her into the kitchen.

"Look,'' he whispered, ducking his head behind a cupboard door and pulling Prudence inside with him, "just go along with everything I say, okay?''

"Oh, brother,'' Prudence whispered back, rolling her eyes at him within the close confines of the cabinet. "So, darling, what are you planning on saying?'' She arched an expectant brow.

"I don't know.'' He frowned. "I'll think of something, though. This is a perfect opportunity to find out a little bit about what they're up to. So,'' he murmured, peeking through the crack where the door was hinged to check on their guests, "just let me do the talking.''

"Oh, this oughta be good," Prudence huffed. "Like the time back in Mrs. Mattson's class when you—"

"Pru? We don't have time to trip down memory lane here, okay?"

"Yeah, yeah, yeah. Just don't get into our sex life again, all right?" Her dimples appeared.

Trent grinned. "Where do you keep the sugar?"

Ducking out of the cabinet, Prudence dragged a canister across the counter and filled the measuring cup to the top. She took a deep breath. "I'm ready if you are."

"I love it when you talk like that." He tweaked her nose.

"Trent." Her voice held a warning.

"I'll be good," he promised, and lifting the cup out of her hands, he led the way back into the living room. "Here we go," Trent said cheerfully as he strode across the colorful area rug and handed Mrs. Skinner the measuring cup, now filled to the top with sugar.

Mrs. Skinner stopped whispering to her husband and her small, beady, raisin-like eyes darted to Trent. "Oh, thank you, ever so much. I'll have Harry return this as soon as we get some grocery shopping done." She smiled benignly at the young couple. "You know how it is, moving into a new place. You never have all the ingredients to prepare a full meal."

"Ah." Trent nodded, and took a seat on the arm of the easy chair where Prudence sat. He dropped a loving arm around her shoulders, and entwined his fingers in her jet-black curls. He loved their silky softness. She'd always had the most incredible hair.

Harry shook his head. "Yeah, seems like all we've been able to find in the boxes we've unpacked is baking stuff." He poked a thumb in Mrs. Skinner's direction. "Gladys loves to bake, as you can probably tell by looking at me."

Gladys patted her husband's spare tire. "Harry's always getting caught with his hand in the cookie jar."

Trent tightened his grip on Prudence's hair and exchanged a silent but significant glance with her. "I'm sure he is."

He could tell that Prudence didn't buy the Skinners' sweet little act any more than he did. That was reassuring. It was good to have a second opinion. He didn't want to go and bust their chops if they were innocent. But, since it was obvious Prudence thought they were a couple of charlatans, too—well, damn the torpedoes and full steam ahead. He would figure out their ruse, and then…slammer time. No more cookies for old Harry.

"Yeah," Harry was saying. "I haven't had a home-cooked meal since we moved here. Probably gonna call that pizza place down on the corner again tonight. Man, I'm tellin' ya—" he thumped his fist against his droopy chest "—if that stuff don't give ya indigestion, I don't know what will."

"Oh, Harry," Gladys chastised, "these kids don't care about your stomach problems."

Trent sat up a little straighter and—gripping one of Prudence's arms in what was becoming their little signal—smiled at Harry. "Oh, sure, we do. Hey, listen. You folks haven't had a home-cooked meal for a long time, why don't you have dinner over here with us tonight?"

Mr. Skinner's watery eyes lit up. "Tonight?" he echoed. Leaning anxiously forward, he sniffed the air and licked his lips. "Something sure smells good, I'll give you that." He nudged Gladys, whose head bobbed in agreement.

This was so perfect, Trent thought, he couldn't have planned it better if he'd tried. "Yeah! Right now," Trent said, his voice loaded with enthusiasm. "Hang on just a second while I check on dinner," he improvised in an effort to seem authentic and loped into the kitchen.

Prudence looked after him, her eyes suddenly wide. "Trent...?" He couldn't be serious. She watched in amazement as he poked his head in the oven and rattled several pots and pans for good measure. Heavens! He *was* serious.

Turning, she stared at the Skinners, and tried to rearrange her dumbfounded expression into some semblance of animated joy. This was just awful. She didn't have anything to give these people. Everything she had that even remotely resembled a meal was either burned or sitting in her garbage pail. The Howatowa Food Mart was surely closed by now. The only option she had was to call the pizza place down on the corner. And, from the sound of Harry's stomach problem, that idea wouldn't sit well with him.

Trent bounded breathlessly back into the living room and took his seat on the arm of the easy chair Prudence occupied. "Coming along nicely," he assured Harry.

Coming along? Last time she'd checked, "dinner" was in the pail under her sink. She was going to kill Trent. Unfortunately, stabbing him in the ribs with her elbows didn't seem to have any effect on him.

"I'm so glad you can stay. It'll be fun." Trent moved his hand to her shoulder and squeezed. "I know what it's like to be new in town and not know anyone. And, since Prudence and I are always looking to expand our social circle, well, why not stay and share our bounty with us? Prudence has been cooking all afternoon, and gosh, from the looks of things in there, we have enough to feed a small army, right, hon?"

Mutely, she nodded. An army of ants, yes.

"Super," Harry cried. "Let's eat. I'm starved."

"Trent!" Smiling brittlely, Prudence reached up and telegraphed a message of her own into his hand with her nails. "Dearest, could I see you in the kitchen for a minute?" She nodded at the older couple. "Please excuse us. We'll be right back." Gripping Trent by the front of his sweater, she dragged him behind her into the kitchen.

Prudence opened the door to her small pantry closet, pulled him inside with her and closed the door after them. They stood nose-to-nose, wedged together among her canned goods.

Wrapping his arms around her waist, Trent pulled her up against his body. "Prudence Mackelroy, this is neither the time nor place—" his low teasing voice filtered through the pitch-blackness "—although, as soon as our guests leave, I'll be happy to pick up where we leave off...." He nuzzled her neck.

"Can it, Trent," Prudence ordered, panic causing her to sustain her grip on the front of his sweater. "Just what in heaven's name are you trying to do? I don't have anything to feed those people!"

"Sure, you do. What about all that food you were fixing when I came home tonight?"

"I burned it! I dropped it on the floor! I threw it away!" Her whispers rose to a fevered pitch.

"Well, get it back. Sort it out," Trent calmly suggested. "Throw it in the microwave. No big deal. I'll wipe off the biscuits and you clean up the salad. Just pick out the dust and stuff and toss it in a bowl. They'll never know the difference."

"Are you out of your mind?" Prudence hissed. "I can't do that! They'll think I'm a horrible hostess."

Loosening her viselike grip on his sweater, Trent pulled her hands into his. "Prudence, who gives a rat's patoot what they think? They're the bad guys, remember?"

"But..."

"No buts."

"But, Trent, what about the stuff I burned?"

"Scrape off the black parts and fix a sauce," he suggested, his voice growing urgent. "If we pour enough gravy over everything, they'll love it. Harry's practically foaming at the mouth now. Listen, they're gonna start wondering what the hell we're doing, hiding here in your pantry closet for so long, so may I suggest that we get out there and start cooking?'' His voice brooked no argument.

"But, Trent," she objected weakly as he pushed open the door and nudged her into the bright kitchen. She blinked up at him, her mouth open to protest.

Grinning, Trent pulled her close and kissed her hard. "One of these days," he whispered against her mouth, "you're going to learn to stop fighting me."

"Uhhh," was all Prudence was able to utter.

"Remember, it's for Uncle Rupert. Now," he urged under his breath, "let's step on it."

"I think we already did that part." Prudence sighed and reached under her sink for the garbage pail.

Chapter Six

"Dinner is served," Prudence sang out cheerily, striving to mask her quaking voice with serene domesticity.

Waving with a confidence she was nowhere near feeling, she beckoned the Skinners and Trent to join her in the minuscule breakfast nook. Her heart thrummed mercilessly and an uneasy feeling of dread settled like a thick, wool scarf in her throat. For the love of Mike, what on earth was she doing playing hostess to a couple of criminals? she wondered, beginning to question her sanity.

As the older couple shuffled into her kitchen, Prudence took a step back and nervously studied her reflection in the darkened panes of her ocean-view window. She almost didn't recognize herself anymore. She shifted her gaze back to the Skinners and watched as Trent hustled them into their seats.

Too late to back out now. Her stomach jumped into a tangled knot.

"Right over there," Trent said, pointing to her little wooden table and chairs.

"Yes, just make yourselves at home," she chirped.

Oh, heaven's to Betsy, she thought, beginning to panic in

earnest, they were never going to be able to pull this off. Gripping a fistful of her apron, she wadded it between her hands, squeezing until her knuckles turned white.

Her kitchen was way too small. They would all have to sit so—she swallowed—close together. The Skinners would see right through them, she was sure. They would never believe that she and Trent were in love. No telling what they would do when they figured out that she and Trent were spying on them. Leaning against the edge of the counter for support, she shot a worried look up at Trent.

Reaching out, he stroked her cheek and smiled reassuringly, as if he could sense what a strain this whole ordeal was for her.

"Here you go," Trent said, steering Mrs. Skinner into her chair, as he calmly played the part of host in this nightmare.

Yes, she decided as she took a steadying breath and tentatively returned his smile. Trent was there.... Everything would be all right. His strong, unflappable demeanor began to relax her. He seemed so confident and unafraid—almost as if he were enjoying himself. Releasing her steely clasp on her apron, she smoothed it over her hips.

Gracious, she was being so silly. Surely she had more to fear from eating the meal that she and Trent had rescued from her kitchen floor, than any dastardly plot the Skinners were hatching.

If she was going to survive this evening, she needed to get a grip. To put things into perspective. The fact of the matter was—she told herself as she reached for her mental boot straps—they were on a mission. She was helping Trent save her friends from disaster. The good guys against the bad guys, battling the forces of evil, so to speak.

Slowly, Prudence began to feel a bud of excitement start to bloom in her stomach. The theme to "The Lone Ranger" reared back and galloped through her mind. Yes! This was for a good cause.

Lumpy gravy and all.

Remembering her arrangement with Trent, she decided it was time to throw herself into the moment for the well-being of Rupert and friends. She affected her best look of loving adoration at Trent as he helped her into her seat.

Since she had only two kitchen chairs, she and Trent would be sharing an old wooden crate that he'd dragged in from under the back porch. It was damp and moldy, but it would serve the purpose. As it was, the four of them were practically sitting in each other's laps.

"Something sure smells dynamite," Harry Skinner crowed, as he squeezed into the chair next to his wife at the other side of the table.

"You could say that," Prudence murmured, peeking up at Trent as he settled himself beside her on the old crate.

Trent looked as if he were trying not to laugh. Fighting the urge to laugh herself, she nudged him with her elbow. He nudged her back.

Trent reached for the rubbery roast and peeked under the mountain of parsley they'd used to disguise it. "Would Willard be interested in some pot roast, Mrs. Skinner?" he asked, referring to the hound as it belched dramatically from somewhere under the table.

"Please, call me Gladys, and my husband Harry," she instructed. "You could give Willard some if you like. I just hope it won't come right back up." Her trill of laughter filled the small kitchen.

"Well, we can't have that," Trent quickly said and smiled. Picking up the carving knife, he valiantly attempted to saw apart several chunks of the leathery meat. Small beads of sweat began to form on his forehead as he labored. "Nope... Can't..." he grunted cheerfully, struggling to appear tranquil, "have...that."

"No," Prudence murmured, biting the inside of her cheek. Although, with their luck, the dog wouldn't be the only one with stomach problems by the end of the meal. Lifting the bowl of carrots, she passed it to Gladys. "Baby carrots?"

"Yes, thank you." The older woman peered into the serving dish. "How interesting," she commented with a raised brow. She scooped a pile of the black-and-orange hockey pucks onto her plate, then passed it to her husband.

Having finished his carving duties, Trent loaded his own plate with a spoonful of the burned vegetables. "Nobody makes Cajun-style carrots like my Prudence," he said. "And the potatoes?" He nodded chummily at their guests. "Pan blackened." Shaking his head in mock disbelief, he thrust the potatoes at Mrs. Skinner. "I just don't know how she does it."

Prudence could feel Trent's thigh nudging her own, encouraging her to comment. Unfortunately, a wild fit of hysterical laughter crowded into her throat, making conversation difficult. Cajun-style carrots?

"I must have the recipe, then," Gladys said, helping herself to some Cajun-style potatoes and a slice of Cajun-style roast.

"Oh, it's just something Prudence threw together, right, honey?" Trent said conversationally, as he buttered his biscuit.

"Ha!" Prudence squeaked and coughed. "Threw together. Yes." She buried her head for a moment against Trent's shoulder in an effort to regain her composure.

"That's what I love about my Prudence. So modest," Trent said, patting the side of her head and grinning. "The woman fairly sizzles in the kitchen."

"Ahh-haaa." Prudence laughed hysterically into his shoulder. This was too much. She was going to lose it. "Trent, please," she begged, clutching a fistful of his sleeve and dabbing her eyes. It wouldn't do to die laughing. Not yet, anyway. Not until the Skinners were behind bars. Sniffing, she looked up at the older couple.

"She hates it when I brag," Trent explained and smiled benignly.

Harry only nodded, for he was too busy chewing his mouthful of pot roast to participate in the conversation with any more than an occasional grunt. Lips smacking loudly, he arched a quizzical, bloodshot glance at his wife as his jowls bounced energetically in the workout of a lifetime. Gladys returned his curious stare and shrugged lightly, quite busy with her own chewing efforts.

At long last able to swallow, Gladys dabbed at her lips with a napkin and beamed at Prudence. "So," she commented when she could finally speak, "you two are going to be getting married?"

Trent nodded, Prudence shook her head, and they both spoke in unison.

"Oh, yes."

"Oh, no."

Prudence looked at Trent in consternation. It wasn't really necessary for the Skinners to believe that they were engaged, was it? Certainly, the fact that they were dating should satisfy their curiosity about why Trent would be spending so much time in her apartment.

"Oh, uh, well, not right away, I mean," Prudence gushed and did her best to look enthralled with Trent. He'd said to follow his lead. He must have a reason for wanting the older couple to believe that marriage loomed on the horizon for them.

Trent encircled her shoulders with his arm and kissed the top of her head. "Not this week, anyway," he said in a possessive tone. "But, I'll tell you this much—to let anyone who can cook like Prudence get away would be a tragedy. Right, Harry?"

Jaws still grinding away, Harry sent Trent a watery-eyed nod. "Mumph," he grunted, and went back to his noisy lip smacking.

Heavens, Prudence thought. It was surprising that she hadn't heard Harry eating through the wall that divided their apartments. She'd never heard anyone slurp and smack at their food with quite such gusto.

"Eat up, Harry. There's plenty more where that came

from.'' Trent grabbed a cleaver from the counter, chopped off another huge chunk of pot roast and lobbed it onto Harry's plate where it landed with a dull thud. "Yeah," he continued conversationally, "we'd like to have a bunch of kids, right off the bat, but in today's world, well, that can cost a bundle. And we're not made of money." He laughed easily and refilled the older man's water glass.

Prudence regarded Trent with interest. Did he really want a bunch of kids? she wondered in surprise at the coincidence. She hadn't known that he wanted a big family. If that was the case, why hadn't he married and had a child or two? For some strange reason, she was suddenly glad that he hadn't.

As Trent reached across the table, his movements created a fluttering in her stomach and she considered the possibility of having his baby. The very idea caused a myriad of sexy images to swirl in her mind. If his devotion to his Uncle Rupert was any indication, he would make a pretty wonderful father.

Good grief. What was she doing, thinking about having Trent's baby? A little bundle of terror to call her own? She darted a look up into his handsome face as he elaborated on his family plans to her neighbors. Was she crazy?

Maybe. Maybe not.

So, what else was new? She sighed to herself. She never knew which end was up when it came to dealing with Trent.

"That's why—" Trent set the pitcher down and pulled Prudence close "—we're trying to figure out a way to make some extra money."

A light clicked on in Prudence's head as she began to understand the direction of his conversation. So, that was what Trent was doing. Fishing for investment advice. Pretty sharp. Jumping to his aid, she threaded her arm through his.

"Ah. Extra money. Yes! We are interested in ways to make extra money. That's for sure," she ad-libbed and nodded vigorously.

She looked up at Trent with admiration in her eyes. His

gaze reflected his admiration of her and suddenly Prudence wasn't certain if she were pretending or not.

Trent turned to the Skinners. "We've been thinking about investing our money in some way or other...." He let the sentence hang uncomfortably in the air.

"Mmmph," Harry grunted and held his hand up to indicate that he was still chewing and most likely would be for a while.

Unable to take the lengthy, lip-smacking silence, Prudence jumped in. "I'm partial to...um...uh—" Willard belched from under the table and began to groan "—show dogs as an investment, but Trent, uh, thinks—"

"Too temperamental," Trent supplied.

Prudence smiled at him with relief. "Yes, that's right." She patted Trent's arm enthusiastically. "Animals are a risk. That's the same reason we decided against...ah, pork barrels," she added in a burst of sudden inspiration. She wondered what exactly a pork barrel was. Or, was it pork bellies? It had something to do with investments, she was sure.

The one thing she wasn't sure of was why she was lying through her teeth this way. It was almost as if she and Trent were creating a monster by unleashing her baser instincts. Nibbling her lip, she had to admit that she was enjoying herself far too much.

"What is your opinion on pork barrels?" she asked, narrowing her eyes at Harry.

"Sweetheart, did you know that a pork barrel is a federal appropriation for a local enterprise that—" Trent began, only to be interrupted by Prudence.

"Shh, honey." Prudence waved her hand impatiently at Trent. "Let's hear what Mr. Skinner has to say, okay? Maybe he has a better idea about how we can invest our money." Turning her head back toward Mr. Skinner, she smiled winsomely. "I never liked the pork thing anyway. That was Trent's idea."

Trent's brows shot skyward as he scratched his temple and shrugged.

They waited eagerly for Harry to elaborate. However, for some reason, the older man seemed impervious to the bait. Glancing at his wife, he lifted and dropped his shoulders. ''I don't know, kids,'' he mumbled, and with a huge effort was finally able to swallow. ''There's lots of ways you could go....'' He looked back at Gladys with a meaningful glance. ''Speaking of going...'' He began to get up from his chair.

Gladys shot him a look that drove him back into his seat. ''So,'' she said with great interest, ''you kids will be tying the knot sooner than later?''

Trent nodded enthusiastically. ''Yeah. That's why I'm so interested in, well, you know—'' he winked, steering the conversation back to finances ''—earning power. Cash flow. Gotta make some more money to keep Prudence in the style to which she's become accustomed....''

Prudence glanced around. What style? she wondered.

''Well, that's just fine,'' Gladys replied enthusiastically, pushing her plate back and tossing her napkin on top of it. ''Prudence, you're going to make a wonderful wife. Isn't she, Harry?''

''Mmmph.'' Harry nodded.

''We're going to have to do something for the kids, aren't we, Harry?'' Gladys arched her brows at her husband, telegraphing a silent, mysterious message to him. ''Since they don't have much money and all...''

''Mmmph.'' Harry pushed his plate back and glanced at his watch. ''We should probably be on our way.''

''Oh, no,'' Trent protested. ''You have to stay for dessert. Prudence has been working all day on something special. You'll love it, I promise.''

''It's not Cajun, is it?'' Harry asked suspiciously.

''Oh, no.'' Prudence laughed, frantically searching her brain for something in her cupboards that would qualify as dessert. ''Uh, Trent, honey, why don't you take the Skinners into the living room, while I prepare the...dessert?''

''You got it, babe,'' Trent agreed affably. Lending a hand,

he helped the elderly couple escape from where they'd been wedged behind the table.

"Thanks, babe," Prudence called after them as they all moved toward her living room. What, she wondered frantically, would an English muffin with chocolate sauce taste like?

It seemed to Trent that no matter how broadly he hinted, the Skinners were there to eat, and had decided to leave the financial-investment business for another time. Or for more gullible people, he thought disgruntledly. Did they suspect that he and Prudence were on to them? he wondered as Harry noisily polished off his third helping of the "cake" Prudence had fashioned from toaster tarts and icing.

Were they being too obvious?

Sitting next to Prudence on the couch, he watched as she leaned over and refilled Mrs. Skinner's coffee cup.

Well, if these con artists were on to them, it wasn't because of Prudence's performance. She was wonderful. Perfect. He couldn't have handpicked a better helper in this charade. With her background, she was great with older people, listening to them…making them feel special. Even a couple of crooks like the Skinners. Yeah, Prudence was doing a terrific job.

With the exception of the part about the pork barrel, he thought wryly. It was obvious her knowledge of the stock market was limited, at best.

Maybe he was coming off a little too pushy. Perhaps he should play hard to get for a while—stop hinting to Harry about all the money he hoped to earn through investments. That must be it. He was coming off as too hungry. Most likely, Harry wanted people with the means to play hardball.

It was hard to tell about old Harry. He was an enigma, Trent thought, noting the expensive make of his watch and the size of his wife's diamonds. Obviously, they were financially well-off. Very well-off.

"So," Harry asked, "What do you do for a living, Prudence?"

Trent's ears pricked up. Aha. Harry was interested in Prudence's earning potential.

"I'm a nurse down a the Howatowa Retirement Center."

"No kidding. You're a nurse down there?" Harry exchanged a significant glance with Gladys. "Funny, we didn't see you when we were down there visiting."

Prudence reached out and squeezed Trent's hand. "Oh, well, I was in Alaska all last week on a cruise. I was checking it out for the retirement center."

"My, my, that sounds like an interesting job," Gladys said. "It is."

As Prudence went on to describe her professional duties, her face became animated with love. Watching her, Trent could see how much the seniors she cared for had come to mean to her personally. Memories of the sweet things she used to do for people when she was young, assailed him. It had seemed to him that Prudence was always doing something to ease someone's pain, or to make them smile. She had been an amazing girl and she was an even more amazing woman.

Trent sighed. He hadn't thought it possible to become any more hung up on her than he'd been back in grade school, but, the more he got to know her as a woman, the more he liked her.

"Yes," she was saying, as Trent surfaced from his ruminations and tuned back to the conversation, "right now everyone down at the center is very excited about the arrival of our new director."

Gladys's small, beady black eyes darted to her husband's sagging, watery ones, then back to Prudence. "You're getting a new director?" she asked, her nose twitching with ferret-like interest.

The hairs on the back of Trent's neck stood at attention. Why should Gladys care that the retirement center was getting a new director? Unless she was afraid that the new guy might put a crimp in her swindling style.

"Yes, and not a moment too soon." Prudence nodded and

sighed. Warming to her subject she seemed to forget the real reason they were there. "Every year at this time, we begin planning our annual Howatowa Retirement Center Summer Festival. It's wonderful fun. The seniors make crafts to sell, play music for the locals, and cook and generally just throw a big party."

"A big *party* down at the retirement center?" Gladys exchanged another significant glance with her husband. "Why, that sounds like fun, doesn't it, Harry?"

What the devil was Gladys up to? Trent wondered, eyeing the silent messages the couple sent to each other.

Harry stared pointedly at his watch. "Yeah, Gladys. Sounds great. Well, I hate to eat and run, but we should probably be going, don't you think, dear? I'm sure these kids have better things to do than sit around yacking it up with a couple of old buzzards like us." Standing, he glanced into the bedroom, looked at the hole in the ceiling, then winked at Trent. "Come on, Gladys," he urged, striding toward the front door. "We've taken enough of their time."

Flustered, Gladys grabbed her purse and the sugar they'd borrowed and rushed after her husband. "Well, thank you, kids, so much for your hospitality. It was so nice to let someone else do the—" she smiled weakly "—cooking. And, of course, thank you for the sugar."

"You're welcome," Prudence said, following them as Harry hustled Gladys out the front door.

"Our pleasure," Trent called, watching them disappear with amusement. "They'll be back," he prophesied as Prudence closed the door and shot the bolt in place.

"What makes you so sure?" she asked, sagging against the door, feeling suddenly exhausted.

"They forgot Willard."

"What?" Prudence gasped with a giggle and peered under the coffee table. True enough, the hound was still there, looking distinctly ill. His tail flopped feebly. "Wow," she said, her eyes sparkling with fun, "they must have been in a real hurry to get away from my cooking, to leave poor sick Willy with us. He's like a son to them."

Angling his head toward the animal, Trent nodded. "He looks as if he could be."

Together, they sagged onto her sofa, then leaned against each other and laughed.

"All things considered, I think that went pretty well," Trent said, plucking a lock of her hair off her shoulder and rolling it around his fingers.

"Oh, please," she replied. "If anything, they think we're even weirder than ever." Turning, she smiled up at him, her eyes animated. "First of all, they think we tore a hole in our ceiling having kinky sex, while wearing costumes, no less."

"Ah, come on, Prudie, I'm sure they were young once."

She snorted. "Then, they think I spend the afternoon burning our supper to a crisp while proudly calling it Cajun-style. Cajun," she howled, as the mirth swelled into her throat. "Great save. Strange, but great."

"Thanks."

"Then, we practically beg them to take our money and invest it for us...." Flopping back against the sofa, she giggled. "Yeah, all things considered, I think we managed to convince them that we're certifiable. They're probably on the phone to the funny farm as we speak, seeing about having us hauled away."

Trent looped his arm around her neck and pulled her head onto his chest and playfully ruffled her hair. "Who cares?" He laughed. "At least we established our alibi, and opened the lines of communication."

"I guess, if you consider listening to Harry chew with his mouth wide open, communicating," she said, her cheek resting comfortably on his chest.

Tucking his chin into his shoulder, he looked down at her and smiled. "Do you want to take Willard home, or should I?"

She didn't want to move. It was so pleasant, the two of

them snuggled together this way. Prudence threaded her fingers through her hair, pushing it back over her shoulder. "Mmm," she hummed, comfortably, "I think we should keep him. He may come in handy as a hostage. Although—" she slanted a teasing glance up at Trent "—cleaning up after him would be your job."

"Gee, thanks," Trent said with a grin. "You surprise me. I never would have taken you to be the kidnapper type."

"Yeah, well, considering that I've been spending my off time swinging from the chandelier with you and spying on a couple of extortionists, kidnapping just seems like a natural part of the progression. Daddy would be so proud." Her mouth tilted in a rueful curve.

Reaching up, Trent playfully chucked her under the chin. Their lips were mere inches apart. He felt his pulse pick up speed, just the way it used to, back in the ninth grade. And, just like in the good old days, he wanted to kiss her. More so than ever before, because now he knew how wonderful it could be. But, he thought, leaning away from the danger zone of her alluring mouth, he'd probably better not push his luck. The Skinners weren't here to put on a show for. He needed her help too much to risk blowing it now. As much as he hated to, he nudged Prudence off his chest and stood. The way he was feeling, he knew that he had to put a little distance between them.

"Did you see the way Harry kept thumping his chest?" Trent commented, stretching. "I don't think Cajun food sits too well with him."

"I don't think it sits too well with Willard, either. In fact," Prudence suggested, peeking down at the dog, "I think they might have left him here on purpose."

"You don't suppose—" Trent rubbed his chin thoughtfully. "Naw…"

"What?" Prudence demanded curiously. "Tell me."

Lowering his voice, he leaned toward her. "The dog wouldn't be wearing a wire, would he?"

Prudence laughed. "I think you've been watching too much TV," she whispered.

"Then why are you whispering?"

"Maybe the Skinners watch too much TV, too."

Heads together, both of them peered under the coffee table at Willard. He swung his watery gaze up at them, and groaned.

"Uh, Trent?"

"Huh?"

"I think maybe you'd better get him next door. Fast."

"Why?"

"I think he's gonna—" She stared at the dog in dismay. "Uh-oh."

Trent sighed. "I know, I know. The paper towels are in the kitchen."

Prudence grinned. "You're going to make some lucky kid a great father, one day." For a moment, she allowed the little fantasy to unfold in her mind. She and Trent, herding their brood into church Sunday morning. A brood with blond hair and laughing blue eyes.

No. She shook her head to clear it. Wrong. Her brood had black hair and green eyes. Like their father.

"What are they talking about?" Prudence demanded in a stage whisper. After returning Willard to his rightful owners, Trent had climbed up into her bedroom ceiling and she hadn't seen hide nor hair of him for over an hour.

"Shh." Trent momentarily poked his head out of the hole. "I can't hear with you yammering away."

"I'm not yammering," she retorted huffily.

She watched as his head disappeared once more. Why did he get to have all the fun? she wondered, pacing around her bedroom and wishing she could hear what was going on next door. Trent had pushed her bed far enough out of the way to allow for a ladder. Making up her mind that this whole ordeal was as much her business as his, she climbed up the ladder and hoisted herself into the hole with Trent.

Unfortunately, as she launched herself across his lap, she managed to accidentally kick the ladder over. Together, they watched in dismay as the unwieldy ladder clattered and bounced around for a moment, then fell to the hardwood floor with a resounding crash, taking her bedside lamp and alarm clock with it.

The conversation next door abruptly ceased.

"Way to go," Trent muttered, shifting her to a more comfortable position on his lap.

"Yeah, well, if you didn't want me up here, you should have told me what was going on. I was dying of curiosity down there," she replied in a crabby whisper.

Trent's warm breath tickled her cheek as he sighed in exasperation. "Well, from the sound of things, you're going to die of curiosity up here, too. They stopped talking."

"I just hope we don't die of starvation," Prudence said, gazing ruefully down at the fallen ladder.

"Don't worry, honey," Trent said, playfully nuzzling her neck. "We have our love to keep us alive."

"Then, we're gonna die," Prudence quipped, elbowing him in the ribs.

"Shh." Trent placed a finger over her lips. "They've started talking again."

Leaning toward the Skinners' apartment, they strained to hear their neighbors' conversation.

Trent's chuckle rumbled pleasantly in her ear. "They're talking about us."

"What are they saying?" Prudence asked with a frown.

"They think we're at it again."

"At it?"

"Swinging from the ceiling."

Prudence whapped him on the arm. "Oh, that's just great."

Laughing, Trent lifted her off his lap and settled her on the joist next to him. With a loud yodel, he jumped from the ceiling and landed on her bed.

"Come on, honey!" he shouted roguishly. "The water's fine!"

"I'm gonna kill you," Prudence hissed, mortified.

Madder than a Cajun hen, she jumped from the hole in the attic and landed right on top of Trent.

Chapter Seven

The following morning was a perfect Tuesday in June. From where Prudence stood—gazing out the retirement center's lounge window—she could see a hawk dip and wheel off in the distance over the heavily forested cliffs of the Washington coast. The morning fog had finally burned off, revealing the point where the cloudless blue sky kissed the deeper blue of the ocean. A solitary figure walked on the beach with a dog, and Prudence watched as the animal bounded in the shallow tide, chasing a stick.

The little hillside community of Howatowa was so beautiful at this time of year. Actually, as far as Prudence was concerned, it was quite possibly one of the most beautiful spots on the face of the earth. A lump formed in her throat. It was so sad to think that she might have to leave some day. The windowpane fogged slightly as she sighed. If the economy didn't pick up soon, there might not be a retirement center to employ her anymore, and she would be forced to move to a larger city, like Seattle.

In all her life, Prudence had never known any home other than Howatowa. She'd planned on staying here forever. Marrying her dream man, raising her family and ultimately, growing old, right here in this little corner of the world. She loved this town with all her heart. Blinking rapidly against the bright sunlight and the unshed tears that suddenly brimmed in her eyes, she turned and smiled at the little group that sat across the room from her in their usual spot, playing a board game.

If anything could cheer her up, it was social hour with Rupert and the gang. Pouring herself a cup of fragrant coffee, she listened with a smile to the silly antics of the Monopoly-playing bunch.

"Do not pass Go, do not collect two hundred dollars," Clementine crowed in her foggy baritone. With great fanfare, she grabbed Norvil's dog and trotted it off to jail. "Stay, little doggy," she commanded, then tsked sadly at Norvil.

"Yeah," Norvil grumbled, fuming. "You just wait, old girl."

Clementine guffawed. "Aw, you're not gonna turn the board over again, are ya, Norvie?"

"I don't know," Norvil snapped. "Wait and see."

"Oh," Clementine croaked in amusement.

Prudence carried her coffee cup back over to the window and let the streaming sun relax her muscles for the remainder of her break. The waves crashed up onto the shore, and she could see the man and his dog leaving the beach. Taking a sip of her coffee, she noticed that the man had blond hair—which, of course, reminded her of Trent. Unfortunately, it seemed lately that everything reminded her of Trent.

Stretching languidly, she sank onto the black leather couch and smiled to herself. He'd been really great last night at their impromptu dinner party with the Skinners. She had to admire the way he was able to think on his feet. After all these years, she was finally beginning to appreciate the way his mind worked. And, as much as she hated to admit it, she'd really gotten a kick out of helping him.

Much to her chagrin, she found she was actually looking

forward to the next time they could get together and play amateur detective.

But, was that what she was really looking forward to? she wondered, reflecting on the time she'd been spending with Trent. As much as she tried to fight it, she knew she was losing the battle against her attraction to Trent.

She rested the rim of the coffee cup against her lips, and continued to stare out, unseeing, over the endless expanse of ocean.

For reasons of self-preservation, she tried to remind herself that all this kissing and hugging and hand-holding was only for show. He didn't really mean any of it. It was all just an act.

But, however true that might be, a part of her wanted to pretend that he was kissing her because he found her attractive now, as a woman, unlike the prissy little girl he'd teased in grade school.

Thinking back, she couldn't really blame him for some of the ways he'd treated her when they were children. She knew that she used to come off as holier-than-thou more often than not.

What he didn't realize was that her prim attitude was a defense mechanism. It had covered up her insecurities. Insecurities about not being as cool and hip as all the other kids. About not being as cool as him. For heaven's sake, it was tough to be hip with cheeks so chubby she looked like a squirrel gathering nuts. And her hair had been incredibly unmanageable. Yes, the Miss Goody Two-Shoes act had protected her from getting too close to people like Trent—people who challenged her control. For, if there was one thing that Prudence had always liked, it was staying in control.

No wonder she was such a mess these days. With Trent, she felt completely out of control. Closing her eyes, she pulled her lower lip between her teeth and thought about his kiss. If she wasn't mistaken, she thought maybe he had been a little out of control, too, if his ragged breathing had been any indication.

A loud outburst from across the room drew her from her woolgathering.

"Now, Rupert, you put that back," Hetta trilled, slapping his hands away from the bank. "I see what you're up to, so just knock it off," she huffed. "If you keep cheating, Norvil will flip the board. Right, Norvil?"

Norvil had dozed off.

"Sorry, toots." Rupert had the decency to look contrite. "You know me, always trying to get rich quick."

"Well, stop or Norvil will just have to be the banker. Right, Norvil?"

Norvil's mouth dropped open as he began to snore.

Rupert grinned. "Never mind. I'll be living on a Park Place of my own, when my ship comes in."

"Yeah," Clementine agreed. "Won't it be great to move out of the retirement center and live in style? I'm gonna buy a place of my own, and run a—" she shot a covert look at Prudence and lowered her voice "—candy store. I always wanted one as a kid. People who come to the new resort will want candy, for sure."

Her break finished, Prudence stood and carried her mug over to the little sink by the coffee machine and thoughtfully rinsed it, as she listened to the folks carry on.

"It's true, Clementine," Hetta was saying, "you make great fudge."

Clementine's raspy voice rang out. "Speaking of my fudge, I think I'll whip up a batch for the retirement center's Summer Festival next month. I can test-market it that way."

"That's a good idea." Rupert nodded and grinned as he pilfered the sleeping Norvil's properties while the man's head bobbed in slumber. "The middle of July will be here before you know it. We don't have much time to get our act together. The sooner that new director of ours shows up to give us a hand planning this thing, the better. We need to get moving if we're gonna get everything done," he proclaimed, scooting several of Norvil's hotels onto his property.

Prudence bit back a smile. She could see where Trent had gotten some of his skulduggery.

"Yeah," Rupert drawled, lazily scratching his chest, "I've been so busy thinking about this resort opportunity, and my new mansion, I've plum forgotten about the Summer Festival. I'm gonna have to whittle a pile of those whistles I make every year for the kids."

"I thought I'd knit some toilet-paper cozies," Hetta interjected.

With a noisy snort, Norvil woke up. "Oh, for the love of Pete, who wants to keep their toilet paper cozy?" he asked grumpily.

"Lots of people love my ballerina cozies," Hetta snapped defensively. "What else are you going to do, Rupert?"

"Well, as usual, I'm running the bingo and poker games."

"Well, Rupert, I can only hope that you don't rob the good folks of Howatowa half blind, the way you do your closest friends," Clementine told him.

"What?" Rupert asked, giving her a look of wide-eyed innocence.

Silent mirth bubbled into Prudence's throat as she turned and leaned against the counter. She watched them with a feeling of love, so poignant, she almost felt as if she was going to burst. They were all so special and wonderful. How could someone like the Skinners take advantage of such lovely people? she wondered, feeling a surge of anger overtake her.

As a pair of strong masculine arms circled her waist, Prudence suddenly found herself enveloped in Trent's embrace. Standing behind her, he pulled her back against his chest and noisily nuzzled her neck. Remember, she warned herself as a giddy feeling of delight swept over her, he's only putting on a display for his grinning audience.

"Oh, hi," Prudence she said breezily, as if this type of thing happened to her every day. She tried to swallow her feelings of pleasure at his embrace. It was the hardest thing she'd ever had to do: steel herself emotionally, and at the same time—for the benefit of their audience—appear enraptured by his surprise visit.

Unfortunately for her sanity, as she leaned into Trent's solid chest, Prudence couldn't tell where the act left off and reality began.

"Gracious, you snuck up on me," she chided, in her most loving girlfriend-like voice. "I didn't expect to see you this morning." Don't be quite so thrilled to see him, she silently scolded herself. He doesn't have dark curly hair.

"Mmm," Trent murmured into her neck. "I've missed you."

"Yoo-hoo," Hetta screeched teasingly. "I'll take some of that."

"Not now, Hetta." Trent tossed a flirtatious wink in her direction, "Prudence might get jealous. I can't have two beautiful women fighting over me."

Clementine guffawed. "Ah, let 'em at it, I say. And, when they've done each other in, I'll be waiting there for ya, honey. You can help me run my candy store."

"Tempting as that might be, I think I have all the sugar I can handle right here in my arms. Right, sweetheart?" He growled playfully.

Prudence groaned. Yuck. This conversation was giving her cavities. Trent nipped her lightly on the neck. And goose bumps. And shivers. And butterflies... Why did she always have to suffer from such a maelstrom of contradictions whenever she was around him?

Be strong, she sternly instructed herself as she fought to remember that this was simply for the good of the community. Turning in Trent's embrace she looped her arms around his neck. "So," she asked cheekily, "what are you doing here?"

Backing her up against the kitchenette counter, Trent pressed into her and nipped at her ear. "Just thought I'd stop by and see if the Skinners were here,'' he whispered, letting his hands rove over her hips.

Her heart stampeded wildly around her rib cage. "Not yet," she whispered back, withdrawing his hands to the small of her back where they belonged.

"Party pooper," he teased, bringing his grin to hover just slightly above hers.

He looked deeply into her eyes, and she felt an uncontrollable thrill race up and down her body like the lights around a marquee. "Trent," she murmured breathlessly against his sexy, sculpted lips, "I'm at work, for heaven's sake."

The crescents at the corners of his mouth deepened wickedly. "Live a little," he instructed, before claiming her lips with his.

Tilting her head, she lost herself in the moment and allowed Trent to devour her with his hungry, demanding kiss. Her mind swam with delicious dizziness as he filled his hands with her hair and bent her back over the counter. He was demanding and commanding and—oh, Prudence thought muzzily, all grown-up.

Her knees felt weak as she splayed her palms across the firm wall of his chest, then ran her hands up to his shoulders and back down to his strong biceps. There, she gripped his arms and hung on for dear life.

Trent was in control. And the funny thing was, for the first time in her life, she didn't care.

Enthusiastic hoots and catcalls came from the group at the table.

"Ah-hem. Excuse me." A strange man's voice penetrated her hazy passion to reach Prudence from somewhere over Trent's shoulder. Then he cleared his throat in an attempt to get some attention. "Could someone please tell me where I could find Prudence Mackelroy? I'm Leonard Frederick, the new director…?"

Prudence closed her eyes and groaned. Great, just the kind of impression she wanted to make on her new boss—making out with her boyfriend at work, while a group of eager voyeurs cheered her on.

Pushing away from Trent, she took a shaky step back and smoothed the white uniform she wore with the clammy palms of her hands. With a rueful look at Trent, she pasted a smile on her now flaming-red face and did her best to look professional.

"I'm Prudence Mackelroy," she said calmly, as she turned to face her new employer. She could only hope, as she swung her gaze to collide with his, that he was a…nice…person.

Sure that her heart had stopped beating, the only thing that kept Prudence from slipping to the floor from shock was Trent's strong arms at her waist. For there, standing before her in all his glory was what Prudence was simply positive had to be the answer to her prayer.

Leonard Frederick not only had dark, curly black hair and a mustache, he also had large green eyes that were presently sparkling.

Unfortunately, it was the sparkle of marked disapproval.

Wearily, Prudence let herself into her apartment and slammed the door. Gathering the mail from the floor beneath the slot, she tossed it on the hall table and slogged dispiritedly toward her kitchen. Trent would be by in a little while to spy on the Skinners, so, until then, she wanted to take some time to unwind. To relax. To mentally kick herself around the block a few dozen times.

What a day. What a horrible, awful, terrible…hellish day. How could she have been so stupid? Finally, after all these years, she gets the answer to her prayers, and what is she doing? Why, she's making out with Trent Tanner, the scourge of her childhood, of course.

For years, the wildest thing she had ever done at work was the crossword puzzle, and now, on the most important day of not only her career, but her life, she'd been playing the part of Howatowa Hussy, and loving it.

Trent had certainly done nothing to further her cause with the father of her twins. The possessive way he'd held her and introduced himself as "Prudence's better half..."

"Oh," she groaned and flopped onto her sofa, kicking her shoes halfway across the room. Leonard would simply never believe her when she told him that *he* was the answer to her prayer, and that they would be getting married and having a bunch of children. She buried her head in a cushion and screamed in frustration.

Although, she had to admit, getting close to Leonard—close enough to tell him about his destiny, at any rate—would take some doing. He certainly wasn't the warmest person she'd ever met. Or the most forgiving, she thought—grimacing at the way he'd suggested that Trent be on his way so that he could get down to business. Kind of a brassy thing to do, considering—boss or not— he was the new kid on the block.

Oh, well. Probably, underneath all that rather stodgy, condescending, no-nonsense attitude of his, he was a wonderful person. A wonderful person who would make a wonderful husband and father. She just needed to take some time to get to know him. And to let him see her in a positive light. Just as soon as he realized that they were two peas in a pod, he would fall down on bended knee and beg her to marry him.

Maybe, she thought, trying to come up with some sort of plan that would further her cause with Leonard, maybe she could persuade Trent to stage a big breakup scene with her, once they'd solved this phony land-scam problem. That would kill several birds with one stone if they did it down at the retirement center. The folks would get off the Prudence-and-Trent bandwagon, and Leonard would see her as she really was: a rigid, straitlaced, no-fun kind of gal. Just like him. Before she knew it, she would be Mrs. Leonard Frederick.

She writhed uncomfortably in her seat on the couch. Why was the picture so dismal? she wondered. After all, it was virtually everything she'd ever wanted.

So, why wasn't she jumping up and down with joy? She

should be thanking God for her answered prayer, but for some reason, she was feeling vaguely blue. "Why?" she whispered, sending her question up past her ceiling and beyond the blue Howatowa skies to heaven.

The chime of the doorbell was her only answer.

"Hi, honey, I'm home!" Trent shouted in his usual jovial style, as she answered the door. "And I've missed you something fierce," he said loudly for the Skinners' benefit.

Reaching for Prudence, Trent dragged her into his arms and settled his mouth over her luscious lips, the way he'd been dreaming of doing all day long. Oh, man, how the thoughts of this woman had interfered with his concentration.

He'd only heard half of what most of the state bureaus and agencies had told him about the Skinners and their nonexistent business. Unfortunately, on more than one occasion, he'd found himself "uh-hmming" into the phone, where his mind was busy fantasizing about the moment he would take Prudence into his arms and kiss her into oblivion. Fantasizing about the moment she would melt into his embrace and return his kiss with the same passion she had the night he'd fallen through her ceiling.

Only, it wasn't happening at all the way he'd hoped.

Pulling back, Prudence placed her hands on his chest. "Trent," she murmured, and sliding her hands to his, tugged him into her apartment and closed the door. She turned, and without waiting to see if he would follow, shuffled into her living room and sank onto her sofa.

"Hey," he said, taking the seat next to her. He tilted her chin up and peered into her eyes. "Why are you so blue?"

Heaving a heartfelt sigh, Prudence lifted her large emerald eyes to his. "You're going to think I'm nuts."

"Try me," he coaxed. Reaching up, he circled the back of her neck with his fingers and began to rub. He would never think Prudence was nuts. Why, she was one of the sanest people he'd ever met.

"Well," she began, closing her eyes to his ministrations,

"it all started a long time ago. Before my folks passed away, actually. I think my mother and father's fondest wish was that I would find a nice man to settle down and have a family with. They knew that they wouldn't be around forever. And, since I'm an only child, I think they worried about me in that regard." She opened her eyes and looked at Trent. "I'm not telling you this to make you feel sorry for me," she assured him.

"I know," Trent said. She could tell him anything, he thought, feeling suddenly very thankful that she felt comfortable enough to confide in him this way. And, of course, he had to admit, he liked the direction the conversation was taking. He infused what he hoped was a great deal of compassion into his expression and nodded for her to continue.

"Anyway, I did some dating, but never with much luck. For some reason, the men I went out with never seemed to meet my expectations."

Trent nodded vigorously. He knew the feeling. Hell, maybe the reason none of the women he'd dated worked out, was because he and Prudence were meant to be together. Stranger things had happened. Maybe, he thought, excitement tightening his chest, just maybe she'd never been satisfied with her dating life because she'd been comparing everyone to him. His heart began to pound.

Taking a deep breath, he continued to gently massage her neck and shoulders. "Go on," he encouraged, smiling tenderly.

She bestowed on him a tremulous smile that nearly busted his heart in two.

"So, I made a list of all the things I wanted in a man. I was very specific. Right down to the color of his hair and his eyes."

Nodding his head, he tightened his fingers on her shoulders, as hope began to burn in his belly. As a thrilling jolt of desire traveled through his body causing his flesh to fairly sing with delight, he leaned imperceptibly closer to the woman of his future and hung on her every word.

"And," she continued, "each night as I said my prayers, I would ask God to send me the man of my dreams. And, when you fell through the ceiling and landed on my bed, just as I was asking for the twins..."

Trent frowned. She wanted two men?

Noting his perplexed expression, she explained, "My future children, MaryJane and John, named for my mother and father."

"Oh," he breathed in relief. Twins sounded great to him. Shucks, the more the merrier.

"At any rate, just as I was asking for the twins and describing their father—" swallowing, she looked up at him "—I always described their father—"

Trent grinned headily.

"You fell through the ceiling."

So, that was it, he thought, his chest swelling with pride, his eyes glazing over as he pondered the enormity of her words. He was the answer to her prayer! That was why she hadn't screamed bloody murder when he'd landed on her bed. No wonder she'd acted so strangely when he'd grilled her about the whereabouts of her husband. No wonder she hadn't run to the phone and called the police. He grinned. Now he understood.

And, if possible, her little story endeared her more to him than ever before. He was one lucky guy. How many men could actually claim that they were the answer to a woman's *prayer?*

Then again... Something Prudence was saying suddenly stilled his fingers as they worked on the muscles in her neck.

"And you took off your hat and I recognized you. So, that's how I knew that there was no way on God's green earth that you were the answer to my prayer."

His heart sank like a lead zeppelin. What? What was she saying? Trent focused his gaze on her lips as they moved, but it was almost as if she was speaking a foreign language. It almost sounded like she'd said he *wasn't* the answer to her prayer.

"So, of course, being that he has dark curly hair and a mustache, and of course, green eyes, just like Papa, well, that's when I knew."

"Knew what?" Trent asked dully, still trying to catch up with what she was saying.

"That Leonard Frederick was the answer to my prayer, of course. My future husband. The father of my children."

Stunned beyond comment, Trent could simply stare at her. Surely she jested. Leonard Frederick, the father of her children? He had to bite his tongue to keep from laughing out loud. It didn't take a rocket scientist to notice that Leonard Frederick was a complete geek. In Trent's opinion, Leonard ranked right down there on the food chain with the Skinners.

Oh, maybe he wasn't a crook or anything, but he was a simpering, snobbish, priggish little weasel, just the same.

"Leonard Frederick?" Scooting back slightly in his seat, Trent could see that Prudence was serious. Something about her earnest expression made him want to go weasel hunting. She preferred a wuss like Frederick to a regular guy like him? Why? Unable to stop himself, he asked the question that begged to be asked.

"What could you possibly want with a stuffed shirt like him? And what on earth makes you so sure he's the answer to your prayer?"

Prudence set her chin defiantly. "How do you know he's not?"

"Because he's a complete and total twerp, that's why. Come on, Prudie, you'd never be happy with a wuss like him."

"How do you know?"

Because you kiss like a raging tornado, he wanted to shout. Because you're a hot-blooded woman. Far too passionate to waste your life on a guy like Leonard. Because, he wanted to yell, you're mine.

But he didn't.

Instead, he got huffy. "Let me get this straight," he said dryly, leaning all the way back on the sofa's arm and pinning her with his glare. "Every night you'd get down on your knees and say something like, 'Now I lay me down to sleep, I pray the Lord sends me a geek.'"

Okay, so that was a low blow, but hell, she'd just gutted him like he was some kind of fish. At the moment, he didn't have what it took to wish the happy couple his best.

"No," Prudence snapped. "I asked for a husband with dark hair and a mustache and green eyes. Like Papa. Like Leonard." Saying it out loud made her realize just how ridiculous her wish list was. But, as usual, something about the arrogant look on Trent's face made it impossible to back down.

"Oh," Trent said, throwing his hands up. "Well, why didn't you say so? Dark curly hair. Of course. And a mustache." There was a sarcastic edge to his voice that he couldn't seem to control. "I suppose profoundly deep, heartfelt, nonsuperficial qualities like that would be enough to satisfy even the choosiest woman on a quest for a mate."

His barbs had hit their mark, for Prudence looked ready to jump at him and pummel him into a pulp. "Leonard does not strike me as a superficial man," she retorted angrily.

Shaking his head, Trent just looked at her. "Whatever." He stood. He had to get out of here. "I'll see you later. I have things to do."

Prudence popped the top off the aspirin bottle and shook two tablets into her hand as she stared morosely at her reflection in the bathroom mirror. Thanks to Trent, her awful, hideous day had gone from bad to worse. And, the pitiful thing was, she couldn't even lock herself in her bedroom and lick her wounds because he was in there, eavesdropping on her neighbors.

Gosh, darn it, anyway. Why had she told him about Leonard being the answer to her prayer? She should have known better than to trust Trent-the-Terror with her innermost secrets and desires. Slapping the aspirins into her mouth, she chased them down with a glass of water and shoved the bottle back into her medicine cabinet. Oh, it was so humiliating. He'd looked at her as if she'd finally gone over the waterfall. Had she?

Was she really being as foolish as he'd made her feel? No. How could it be foolish to hope that God would answer her prayer with the man of her dreams? Certainly there was nothing silly about that. Who was he to laugh at her destiny? If Leonard Frederick was the man for her, then she would happily accept her lot in life.

True, she scarcely knew the man. However, she realized that first impressions were sometimes misleading. She would give Leonard the benefit of the doubt. Surely he wasn't as bad as Trent seemed to think he was. No. God would never send a— what was it Trent had called him?—a wuss to marry her and father her children.

She grinned around the pounding in her temples. Trent had muttered something under his breath all the way into her bedroom and up the ladder. She hadn't caught everything he'd said, but it had sounded a lot like "Meet John and MaryJane Wuss, the Wuss twins."

At the clattering that came from her bedroom, Prudence shut the medicine cabinet and went to find out what Trent had discovered. Entering the bedroom, she found him dusting himself off and grinning at her. Apparently he had forgiven her for her announcement that she would most likely be settling down with a "wuss like Leonard."

She was relieved. Trent's opinion of her had come to mean a lot. More, actually, than she was willing to admit.

"Guess what I overheard?" he asked, his deep blue eyes sparkling with excitement. "The Skinners are going out to dinner this Friday night, down at the Howatowa Café."

"Oh?" Prudence lifted her brows. Was she missing something?

Laughing, he correctly interpreted her confused expression.

"They're meeting Rupert there for dinner. So, I figure we should go out this Friday night, too," he exclaimed.

"I'm not going to the Howatowa Café." Prudence shook her head warily.

"Why not?" Trent frowned.

"Because that's the only restaurant in town these days. What if Leonard Frederick is there?"

"Prudence, forget that little dork for a minute, will you? We have more important things on our plate right now than your budding romance with that twerp."

"That twerp, as you so indelicately put it, just so happens to be the answer to my prayer," she said huffily. "So, I would appreciate it if you would please not jeopardize something that I have waited for for nearly half my life now."

Trent sighed and dragged a frustrated hand over his face. "Okay, okay. No problem. We'll wear disguises. I'll make the arrangements and meet you here right after work on Friday."

"Costumes? Oh, Trent, please. Remember what happened the last time you wore a costume? Your mustache fell off, for crying out loud. The Skinners already think we're out of our ever-lovin' minds. And, if by chance Leonard happens to be there, I don't want him seeing us and getting the wrong idea." She eyed him sternly. "You seem to forget that he's not just the answer to my prayer, he's also my boss. I don't want to lose my job because of some harebrained scheme of yours."

"Prudence, don't worry. We'll go, we'll sit in a dark corner, we'll have dinner, we'll listen to their plans, and then we'll go home. Easy as one, two, three. Hey." Reaching forward, he chucked her on the chin. "Stop fretting. If your precious Leonard is there, he will never recognize you. When I'm finished outfitting us," he assured her, "our own mothers wouldn't recognize us."

Flopping facedown on her comforter, Prudence moaned in resignation.

Chapter Eight

"Oh, please," Prudence gasped. Collapsing onto her bed, she proceeded to roll around in a fit of laughter. Tears running down her heavily made-up face, she lolled to one side and peeked up at Trent. "You can't be serious."

It was Friday night, and Trent had just emerged from Prudence's bathroom in his costume—the costume he would wear to the Howatowa Café that evening, to spy on the Skinners.

His face crumpled as he moved through the doorway to her bedroom. "What's wrong?" he asked, looking wounded.

Sitting up, Prudence grabbed a pillow and hugged it to her chest. She pushed her long, disheveled mop of curls away from her eyes and, scrunching her face in a valiant effort to keep from screaming with laughter, said, "It's just that you're so—" she once again lost her battle with glee "—homely!" Her shoulders shook as she buried her face in the pillow. "Ugghhh," she shrieked. "You're hilarious."

"That's not very nice," Trent said, pouting, and turned to look into the mirror that rested on her bureau. "I would never say that to you, even if your panty hose were sagging around your ankles."

Running his hand over his five o'clock shadow, he pondered her opinion. Slowly, his eyes traveled from his curly gray wig, past the large earrings, over the somewhat gaudy brooch pinned securely at his throat, down the floral print dress—which had looked so attractive hanging on the thrift-shop hanger—to his lumpy, slightly lopsided bustline. He had to admit, she had a point. He did not make a very attractive older woman.

But then, who cared? Pretty wasn't the point. No, the point was to change his and Prudence's identity so drastically that the Skinners would never be able to recognize them as they followed the couple to their meeting with his Uncle Rupert at the Howatowa Café.

"I'm sorry." Prudence giggled as contritely as she could manage. "It's just that you're so...busty." Wiping her eyes on a tissue, she leaned back against her headboard and appraised him. "The wig is good, though," she grudgingly admitted with a sniff. "But your makeup is a mess. You shouldn't have laid it on quite so thick. You look like a clown. Here—" she laughed and patted the bed, then held out her hand to him "—sit down."

Sighing, Trent shuffled across the room in his oversized slingback sandals.

Maybe this wasn't such a good idea after all, he thought dispiritedly as he sank down on the edge of Prudence's bed. She crawled across the bed on her knees and sitting beside him, pulled his face between her hands. Then again, he thought, feeling his gut turn a cartwheel as her warm, minty breath tickled his face, maybe this was just what the doctor ordered. His blood began to roar in his ears.

Besides, he rationalized, leaning toward Prudence as she blotted his lips with a tissue, there simply wasn't any other alternative. He couldn't think of a better or more efficient way to overhear what the two swindlers might say to his uncle. Prudence would just have to trust him on this.

"You know you probably should have shaved before you

slathered so much of this orange foundation all over your face," she said, as she tried to repair his other amateur attempts at theatrical makeup. "You look like you have a pretty bad hormone imbalance."

"There wasn't time. I thought if I troweled enough war paint on my face, it would hide everything and no one would recognize me."

"Well, you have a point. No one will recognize you, but everyone will sure be staring." Reaching across his well-padded body, she plucked her makeup bag from her nightstand and began to rummage around inside. "Surely," she muttered, "you could have come up with a better disguise for yourself than this. I mean, come on, Trent. A big, strapping math teacher and football coach like you is going to have a hard time passing yourself off as a little old lady."

"Bertha. Remember I'm Bertha, and you are Bernice. We're sisters."

"Oh, yeah, right." Prudence laughed and began to reapply his lipstick. "Sisters?" Her hand shook with mirth. "Who's gonna buy that?"

Trent grinned. "If anyone asks, we'll just say that you didn't eat your vegetables when we were growing up."

Looping her arms around his neck, Prudence leaned her forehead against his frizzy gray wig and giggled helplessly. Trent loved the sound. Tilting her chin up, he planted a quick kiss on her lips.

Rearing back, she looked at him, taking in the big picture. "Ee-ew," she snorted. "Granny, you're weirding me out."

"Come here," he growled, dragging her across his lap. "I'll weird you out—" He stuffed his face into her neck, and planted a string of noisy kisses across her jaw.

"Trent!" she howled. "I mean, Bertha! Stop it. You're going to mess up all my hard work." Gripping his newly enhanced bustline, she hauled herself into an upright position. "What on earth have you got in there, anyway?" she demanded. "Tennis balls?"

"Rolled-up sweatsocks."

"Did you have to use the whole drawer? I think we've done about as much as we can do with your face. A pair of glasses will help. And, I recommend that you lose several pairs of the sweatsocks."

"No." Trent shook his head as he punched and kneaded his lumpy brassiere into shape. "I'm hoping it will direct people's eyes away from my face, if you get my drift. Listen, we'd better get going." He glanced at the alarm clock on her nightstand. "We don't have much time. I overheard Harry say that they were meeting Rupert at eight. It's already seven-twenty." Pushing himself upright, Trent reached into his satchel and pulled out a gray wig for Prudence. "Here," he instructed, "put this on while I fill you in on our MO."

"Ammo? Trent—" Prudence's eyes grew round "—you're not planning on shooting anyone, are you?"

Laughing, Trent tossed the wig into her lap and fished a pair of spectacles out of the bag for himself. "No, silly. Modus operandi. I think we need a cover story and some background information, just in case we get ourselves backed into a conversational corner, so to speak."

"Oh." Prudence sounded dubious as she energetically stuffed her thick hair up under the wig he'd provided.

"Okay, so, here's the deal," Trent said, flipping his little notebook to the correct page and peering over the edge of his bispecticals. "I wrote a few notes for us here.... Ah, yes. Here they are. Okay, you're Bernice and I'm Bertha. We are the O'Hara sisters."

Her wig firmly in place, she nodded. "Okay. What else?"

"Well, you are a widow with three grandchildren, and another on the way. You just had hip-replacement surgery and are recovering nicely. Your favorite TV show is 'Crime Busters,' you love to garden and you belong to the chess club," he said, beaming at her. "Okay, let's see." He flipped a page. "I'm a divorcée with no grandchildren. I love birds and go bird-watching whenever I can. My son is a computer programmer who married a wonderful girl—"

"Trent," Prudence interrupted impatiently. "I can never remember all this. Do you really think your son will come up in conversation?"

"Uh—" Trent snapped his notebook shut "—good point. Let's go."

The Howatowa Café was a charming, trendy little restaurant that clung to the farthest point west on one of the many cliffs that rose dramatically from the Pacific Ocean. The view from the window was spectacular, making this one of the most popular eateries for miles around. The fact that it was one of the few remaining restaurants in the area didn't hurt business much, either. Beyond the window at the horizon's edge, in a riot of pink and purple streaks, the sun was beginning to make its way toward the briny deep.

It was all so incredibly romantic and beautiful, Prudence suddenly found herself wishing that she were here with Trent on a regular date. In regular clothes. Not in drag, chasing a couple of ne'er-do-wells.

"Trent?"

"Hmm?"

"I'm scared," Prudence admitted, nervously fingering the fringe on her shawl.

"Just relax," he encouraged. "You look fine. You're very dishy for a woman of your years." His eyes roved over her outlandish costume, then out to the main part of the dining room. "Yep," he muttered under his breath. "They're all sitting over there by the window. Come on."

Limping slowly along and clutching his purse, Trent led the way across the room, and much to their waiter's dismay, chose his own table. The table by the Skinners.

"Uh, ma'am," the snobby waiter with an obvious attitude problem impatiently called. "Not that table, please."

"Whyever not?" Bertha-Trent trilled, stuffing himself into the seat and motioning for his sister to follow suit.

Mortified, Prudence kept her head down and prayed that no one would recognize them. So far, the only halfway comforting thing about this debacle was that she hadn't spotted Leonard. Yet. Keeping her shoulders hunched and her face pointed dramatically at the floor, she felt her heart suddenly stop beating as she realized that Trent had lost a pair of sweatsocks. The colorful stripes fairly glowed from beneath their table. So much for an inconspicuous entrance.

Perhaps it would just be best to ignore the sock issue, she decided. With a weak smile at the miffed waiter, Prudence lowered herself into the chair across from Trent.

"Hello?" The arrogant waiter tapped his foot impatiently. "I haven't had a chance to wipe the table down yet," he whined, then threw up his hands. "Oh, go ahead." Tossing several menus on the table, he spun on his heel and stalked off.

"Smile, young man," Trent called gleefully in a shrill tone. "You'd look decidedly more presentable if your nose weren't so far out of joint." Under his breath he muttered, "Pompous jerk. If I weren't such a lady, I'd pound his little—"

"Trent," Prudence hissed, "what are you trying to do?" She peeked over at the table the Skinners and Rupert were occupying. "Will you keep your voice down?"

"Bernice, darling. Remember to call me Bernice."

"I'm Bernice!"

"Whatever. I'd like to rearrange that little twerp's attitude," he growled and picked up his menu. Holding it up to his face, he glanced furtively around. "This is a pretty good table, don't you think? I mean, we can hear almost everything they're saying."

At the moment, the Skinners and Rupert were scanning their menus and discussing the catch of the day.

"Yes." Prudence nodded. "We should probably figure out what we're going to order while they're doing the same thing.

That way, we won't miss out on any of their business conversation.''

"Good idea," Trent agreed and pushed his glasses down to the tip of his nose to better see the selections. "Listen, don't choose any food that makes too much noise, okay? We want to be able to hear everything they're saying."

"No loud food... Hmm." Prudence thoughtfully scanned the menu. "Okay. What foods are quiet?"

"Nothing at all, if Harry's lopping his lips over it," Trent said snidely. He cast a furtive glance over at the Skinners' table as Harry sniffed out the breadbasket and noisily dove in.

Prudence giggled. For some reason, Trent could make even the most nerve-racking ordeal seem fun. She was actually beginning to relax a little and enjoy herself. This wasn't so bad, really. The Skinners weren't even looking at them.

Gazing longingly at the colorful horizon and then back at Prudence, Trent murmured, "Even in that outlandish getup, you are so beautiful against the sunset." He stroked the top of her hand. "Makes me want to kiss you senseless."

Obviously overhearing the odd remark, Mrs. Skinner turned their way and trained her small raisinlike eyes on them, then clutched her throat, obviously shocked. She murmured something to her husband, and Harry fixed his bloodshot gaze on them with interest.

So much for relaxing and enjoying herself, Prudence fumed. Covering her face with her menu, she kicked Trent under the table. "Way to go, Bertha," she hissed.

"Sorry," he mouthed and shrugged sheepishly. "I forgot where I was there, for a moment." Lowering his voice even further, he said, "It's true, though. I still want to haul you across the table and kiss the daylights out of you."

"Oh yeah, now *that* wouldn't draw much attention," she whispered dryly.

However, as much as she hated to admit it, his words thrilled her clear down to the tips of her orthopedic shoes. Again, she tried to remind herself that he was simply in the role-playing mode. He didn't mean he actually wanted to kiss her. He was just in the habit of doing that type of thing in front of the Skinners.

"Please," she begged, attempting to bring her pulse under control, "try to remember which character you're playing at the moment. Right now, you have to pretend to be an old lady, not my boyfriend."

"Who's pretending?" he asked, peeking over his glasses at her.

Grabbing her water tumbler, Prudence took a healthy swig, and fought the breathless feeling of excitement that suddenly had her head in the spin cycle.

Luckily for her, the waiter chose that moment to return to their table. "Ready to order?" he asked them snippily. Apparently Trent's comments about his nose being out of joint had not endeared them to him.

"I'd like the shellfish platter," Prudence decided, doing her best to disguise her voice.

"Oh, no, no, sister dear," Trent yodeled in his falsetto as he smacked her hand. "Shellfish are far too noisy." He arched a pointed brow at her over the top of his menu.

"The…" The waiter looked imperiously down his narrow nose at them. He cleared his throat. "The shell fish are…dead, ma'am. I assure you, they will not be making any noise."

The muscles in Trent's heavily rouged cheek jumped with aggravation. "The lady will have the scrambled eggs with a side of mashed potatoes, and I… Hmm, I think I will have the oatmeal and applesauce. Two coffees," Trent barked.

Deciding to ignore the waiter's contemptuous sneer, Trent shoved the menus into the man's chest with such force, it nearly knocked him over. "Here you go, sonny," he growled menacingly, and scowled after his quickly retreating back.

"Bertha," Prudence hissed, tapping his hand to gain his attention. "Listen up! The Skinners are starting to talk turkey with Rupert."

Trent leaned with Prudence toward the next table, and together they strained to better overhear the thickening plot.

"I don't know, Rupert," Harry was saying. "I think that nephew of yours might figure out what's going on, and muddle up the plans." He rested his droopy, bloodshot gaze on his wife. "I'm tellin' ya, I don't have a good feeling about this part of the plan."

Rupert picked up a bread stick. "No, Harry, stop worrying about my nephew. I'll make sure he stays out of the way. I can handle him," the man assured his dinner companions. "Just leave Trent to me. The way we're going to handle this whole deal, he'll never be able to figure out what's going on."

"Good." Gladys nodded. "Because I don't want to go to all the time and effort to put this thing together, only to have it blow up in our faces. Can you keep your mouth shut around Prudence? I know that she's at the center every day. You'll have to be careful."

"Stop worrying," Rupert said.

Jaws slack, Trent and Prudence stared at each other in stunned disbelief.

"Oh...my...gosh," Prudence gasped, completely horrified. "This is much worse that I thought. They've brainwashed your Uncle Rupert!"

"I can't believe it," Trent whispered, gripping the handle of his purse so tightly, he nearly tore it off.

Leaning forward, Prudence tugged on Trent's wig and brought his ear to her mouth. "You know, I always knew Rupert had a streak of the devil in him, especially when it came to playing cards. But, for heaven's sake, Trent, I never thought he'd be the type to join forces with a pair of swindlers to cheat his friends. He's always had a reputation of being one of the most trustworthy, honest men in town." There was a catch in her throat. "I've always really loved your uncle."

"I know," Trent said dully, his eyes vacant. "Me, too."

Prudence sighed heavily. "Do you think it's too late to talk some sense into him?"

"I don't know, but I'm sure as hell gonna try."

"Oh," Prudence wrung her hands in misery. "Not now, I hope."

"No. Not now."

Reaching across the tabletop, Trent took her hands in his. She looked every bit as sick at heart as he felt. He closed his eyes against the anguish that crowded into his throat. Jeez. The poor guy. Those scumballs really had him in their clutches. They had to figure out a way to get him out of this mess. And soon.

He swallowed and opened his eyes to catch Prudence watching him, her eyes brimming with empathy. If there was even one remotely redeeming aspect of this disgusting evening, it was the way Prudence obviously cared about his family. And, although he knew she was emotionally committed to a future with another kind of man, his heart swelled with love for her.

As he exhaled a frustrated breath, Prudence sympathetically squeezed his hand, running her delicate fingertips over his knuckles. Little did she know, Trent thought ruefully, that his sigh symbolized not only his sadness about his uncle's involvement with the Skinners, but his despair over his own futile involvement with her.

This was a great time to discover that he'd fallen head over slingbacks in love with Preacher Mackelroy's daughter. Oh, he'd always carried a torch for Prudence. But this— This went far deeper than a schoolboy crush. This was the kind of gut feeling that told him he would probably never be able to find real happiness with any other woman for the rest of his life. This was the kind of feeling a full-grown man had for a full-grown woman. It was unlike any other emotion he'd ever felt for her before, and it nearly bowled him over with its potency.

This was turning into a hell of an evening. What a couple of idiots he and his uncle were. Rupert was falling for the oldest trick in the book and he, well, he was falling for a raven-haired angel whose kiss he would never get out of his system.

Shaking his head in an attempt to clear it of these maudlin thoughts, he focused on getting through the evening—just the way he coached his high-school kids to concentrate on finishing a losing game.

"Thank you," he murmured.

"For what?" Prudence whispered.

"For being here for me. For helping. For…caring."

Prudence ducked her head. "Of course, I care."

Yes, Trent thought sadly. But not half as much as he did. A movement at the front door caught his eye. Aw, for the love of Mike. And he'd thought this dismal evening couldn't get any worse.

"Uh-oh," he said and plunged his hands through his hair, only to have the wig slide slightly off. Hastily, he shoved it back on his head.

"What uh-oh?" Prudence demanded, worriedly eyeing the wisps of silky blond hair that peeked out from under the wig's gray curls.

Trent inclined his head at the newcomer as the man followed the waiter toward his table. "The answer to your prayer at twelve o'clock high."

As discreetly as she could, Prudence twisted around to see Leonard making his way toward them. Luckily, he didn't seem to notice them as he arrived at his table.

Even though she was in a horrified muddle over Rupert's duplicity, Prudence couldn't help but notice—in the niggling recesses of her mind—what a rigid, humorless person Leonard was. He even approached dining out as a sterile, precise event. Gracious, she wondered uneasily, did I ask for *that*? She watched as he fastidiously polished both his seat and the table before sitting down. Then, with a savage snap, he unfurled his napkin and tucked it tidily into his lap.

She couldn't ever envision Trent being such a fussbudget. Over the days they'd spent together, she had come to appreciate Trent's easygoing attitude. He made her feel like she could just relax and be herself, faults and all.

Squirming uncomfortably, she darted her gaze back to Trent as he sat there in his gray wig and paste-jewel brooch. Why, she thought in amazement, Trent was twice the man Leonard was. Even in a dress.

Could Leonard really be her lifelong soul mate? The other half of her being? The loving father of her brood?

If that was true, why did her future suddenly look so bleak? Not being one to second-guess an answer to a prayer, she simply had to wonder why she found Trent so much more fun to be with than Leonard. So much more adventurous. Exciting. Funny. Full of life.

And, while it was obvious that Leonard was a hardworking solid citizen, he was also humorless, boring and fussy. If she was going to be spending the rest of her life with him, she would certainly prefer it if he would loosen up once in a while. Laugh a little. Live a little. Surely a simple smile now and then wouldn't shatter his face.

Of course, she amended charitably, she hadn't included those particular characteristics in her prayer, so she couldn't really complain about not getting them. However, she had to wonder why the blond-haired, clean-shaven, blue-eyed Trent possessed the loving, caring, full-of-life-and-laughter characteristics she had admired in her beloved father.

Following the line of her intent gaze, Trent shook his head. "I can't believe that you would even consider marrying that guy," he snorted under his breath just as the waiter arrived with the food.

"Luckily for you," came the waiter's sarcastic reply as he peered down his nose and dropped a bowl of oatmeal in front of Trent, "I'm not available." With a haughty flourish, he tossed the eggs, mashed potatoes and applesauce on the table and disappeared.

Prudence groaned and closed her eyes.

"Shh." Trent put a finger to his lips and leaned toward the Skinners' table. "Listen."

Tucking his napkin under one of his chins, Harry trained

his sad, watery, houndlike gaze on Trent's uncle. "I'm tellin' ya, Rupert, that Prudence can't cook worth beans. I don't think I ever had such heartburn. That nephew of yours is in for a rude awakening."

Rupert laughed.

Prudence gasped and scowled at the insulting man. "What an ingrate," she fumed. "That's the last time I'm having them over for a home-cooked meal...."

Eyes twinkling, Trent pulled his glasses down to the tip of his nose. "Easy, girl. I know you're a good cook."

Sending him a weak smile, Prudence felt suddenly foolish. She was getting way too caught up in this whole mess. As far as she was concerned, it was time to hang up the magnifying glass and call it a night. She wasn't in the mood for mashed potatoes and scrambled eggs, anyway.

"Trent?"

"Hmm?"

"I think I've heard enough for one night."

"Just a sec..." Trent held a finger to his scarlet-smudged lips.

Reaching for her handbag, Gladys stood and leaned toward her companions. "Before we start eating, if you two will excuse me, I'm just going to powder my nose. I'll be right back."

"She's going to powder her nose," Trent hissed. "Let's go!"

"And do what?" Prudence demanded.

"It's a perfect chance to grill her." With that, he was off and running as fast as his furiously bobbing sweatsocks and size-fifteen slingbacks would allow.

With a groan of disbelief, Prudence hoisted herself to her feet and, keeping her face turned away from her future husband and father to her children, followed a man dressed in drag to the women's room so that he could interrogate a little old lady.

What must her father be thinking?

* * *

The following Monday found Prudence standing by the coffee machine in the retirement center's lounge, wondering when Trent was going to make his appearance. Friday night, after they'd spent too many fruitless minutes in the ladies room attempting to interrogate Gladys as she freshened her lipstick, they came up empty-handed once again. The only thing Gladys seemed willing to admit was how much she'd enjoyed the day and weather. Back at the table, they'd fared no better, and after the Skinners and Rupert left, they finally decided to call it a night.

Returning to her place, they traded their costumes in for hot showers and clean clothes. Trent told her that he had to go back to Seattle for the weekend, saying something about wrapping up some fall sports plans he'd made with some of his students.

That was fine, she'd told him. She had a few chores she needed to accomplish, too.

Why, then, had she accomplished her chores in record time and spent the better part of the endless weekend missing him? Until Trent had fallen through her ceiling and landed so unceremoniously on her bed, she'd never had any trouble enjoying weekends—filling her off hours with enjoyable pastimes. She'd never guessed that she would miss him so much.

It seemed that she'd spent the entire weekend wondering how he was doing. And, when she wasn't wondering how he was doing, she was reflecting on what a nice man he'd grown up to be. And how much he seemed to care for his elderly uncle. And, most of all, how nice it was to have a man around the house.

It had been strange and wonderful to hear him thumping around in her shower as she tidied up their disguises and prepared them to go back to the thrift store. She could really get used to the safe and cozy feeling she seemed to slip into whenever he was around. Well, if she could call living on the edge safe and cozy, that is. What was it about Trent that made all these wild escapades seem so...normal? she wondered.

Perhaps it was because above all else, Trent's heart was in the right place. His motives were always pure. Trent Tanner would go to any lengths, sparing no personal expense, to help someone he loved. She really admired that about him.

Where was Leonard's heart? she wondered, suddenly filled with melancholy as she glanced around the lounge for her boss. Surely, if he even had a heart, it was several sizes too small. Just like the Grinch.

"Ah, well." She sighed resignedly and rinsed her mug in the kitchenette's small sink. She'd better stop daydreaming and get to work. Leonard didn't like to see any of his employees standing around, staring off into space.

As confused as she was about the two men she suddenly found in her life, one thing was becoming clear. Leonard was not her idea of a dream come true.

After a torturous, and uncommonly lonely weekend away from Prudence, Trent battled his way out of the usual Monday-morning traffic nightmare in Seattle and finally arrived at the Howatowa Retirement Center. Quietly, he made his way through the building's front door and, tiptoeing through the foyer—in order to avoid Leonard's censure—looked for Prudence.

If he hadn't promised some of his students several months ago that he would help put together an inter-mural basketball league, he never would have left. Following her voice, he made his way toward the lounge. He had only been gone two days, but he couldn't believe how much he'd missed her.

And, now that he saw her, standing in a patch of sunlight that streamed through the window bathing her in a ethereal glow, he knew why. She seemed to be leading a meeting of some sort, with a small group of residents.

Leaning against the archway that led to the large room,

Trent settled in to wait for her, his chest constricting as he watched the poignant scene from his vantage point.

Her tender countenance, as she dealt with the people for whom pain and infirmity were now a way of life, made it so clear that she really cared. She had a capacity to love that boggled his mind. Too bad that love would never extend to him—at least, not the way he wanted it to.

Just watching her, as she smiled so gently at the little cast of characters that made up the retirement center, he wondered morosely how he would ever be able to find the strength to leave again. To go back to a life that did not include this fiery, spunky, loving and completely passionate woman.

He ran an uneasy hand across his face. This uncontrollable dependence on her was starting to unnerve him. But what could he do? It was clear that she would never be able to return his feelings.

Oh, she seemed to like him a lot better now than she did in the ninth grade, but he knew that she would never be able to see beyond their past together—not to mention the curly-haired, mustachioed answer to her prayer—and find a future with him.

No. Prudence had her heart set on old curly, over there. Trent's gaze wandered to Leonard, as he skulked darkly in the background. Man, Trent thought, his eyes narrowing, he detested that guy.

"Okay." Her melodious voice rang out as she checked her clipboard, "Hetta, you are going to be knitting toilet-paper cozies, is that right?"

Norvil snorted rudely.

"Yes," Hetta said, cuffing Norvil on the side of the head.

"Okay." Prudence sighed. "That takes care of the craft portion of the Summer Festival...."

Hmm, so that's what they were talking about. That was okay. He had some time to kill before his meeting with Mart from the State Financial Fraud Section. He didn't really have anything to say to Prudence. He had just wanted to see her lovely face. To hear her voice, sweet and low. To smell the fresh sunshine-and-roses scent of her hair. To run a finger along her smooth jaw and to—if he was very lucky—steal a kiss from those exquisite lips.

"Rupert?" Her tone was somewhat cool, as she addressed his uncle. Trent didn't blame her. Not if what they'd overheard the other night had any validity.

"Yo," Rupert called and waved cheerfully.

"Uh, you're still going to be running the bingo and poker games?" She smiled uncertainly as if she was unsure, now, how to treat the man.

Clearing his throat, Leonard stepped forward. "I don't know if that's the image we want to portray," he interjected with a dark frown. "We are a retirement center, not a gaming facility. I think there are laws against this type of activity." His mustache twitched.

Raising his arms over his head, Trent gripped the doorway molding and leaned forward to watch the byplay between Prudence and her intended.

Criminy, for a woman who'd found her match made in heaven, she sure didn't look very happy with him.

Good. A small smile tugged at his mouth. For the life of him, he just didn't get what Prudence saw in Leonard. Other than the dark-curly-hair-and-mustache thing that he had going for him, the guy was a complete loser. Trent watched the new director's little black mustache twitch in annoyance at something she was saying.

They argued back and forth for a moment, and finally Leonard suggested that they cancel the Summer Festival altogether this year. Prudence and the rest of the residents looked positively horrified.

"Why?" she asked. "We've done it this way for years. In fact, as a child, I always looked forward to playing bingo at the Summer Festival. I don't believe anyone thinks we're trying to turn the retirement center into a casino." She looked

Leonard directly in the eye. "Surely you can't be serious about canceling this year's festival, Mr. Frederick."

If the way she was rubbing her temple was any indication, Trent figured Prudence had the beginnings of a whopper headache.

Leonard shook his head and muttered in disdain. "I don't know," he complained fussily. "I think it will be entirely too much work. These people need their rest. They shouldn't be stressing themselves on a lot of silliness like fudge and cozies and whistles."

Trent snorted loudly in disbelief.

That did it. There was no way in hell that Prudence was going to marry this clown. Over his dead body. As much as he didn't want to interfere with her destiny, he just couldn't bring himself to believe that this guy was the answer to her prayer.

Leonard's head snapped up as he noticed Trent standing in the doorway. "What do you want?" the new director asked curtly.

Trent was here! Prudence's heart sang gloriously as her headache immediately disappeared. Her eyes drank in his virile, masculine presence that seemed to virtually fill the room.

Pushing away from the doorjamb, Trent sauntered into the lounge, like a caged animal waiting for the opportunity to spring. His very demeanor dared the prissy little man to defy him. "I came to see my woman, if it's any of your business," Trent rudely informed him.

Suddenly, Prudence was beyond caring what her future husband thought about her boyfriend visiting her at work. If the pompous wuss didn't like it, well...he could stuff it.

"Make it quick, then," Leonard snapped. "This is not a playground."

Not waiting for him to change his mind, Prudence rushed across the room to Trent and tugged him back through the archway and into the foyer.

"You should leave," she chided, disgustingly happy to see him. "Before Leonard decides to fire me."

"He won't fire you," Trent said, grimly glancing back at the scowling Leonard. "I just wanted to put in an appearance," he told her, his sexy voice low in her ear. "To let you know I'm back."

She was thrilled. "Are you coming over tonight?" she asked, her voice filled with breathless anticipation. She tried to tell herself that the reason she was so excited to see him was because of the things she wanted to tell him—not because she was falling in love with him.

"Yes."

"Good," she whispered excitedly and cast a quick glance over at Rupert, "because I have information."

Trent's eyes crinkled. "Yeah?"

"Uh-hmm. I overheard Rupert and the gang discussing the fact that—" She looked up at Trent and, waving her hands, tried to explain. "It was hard to catch the whole conversation, Trent, but it sounded to me like they were talking about how the Skinners were going to come to the Summer Festival and reveal some sort of— I didn't catch it all, because they started to whisper among themselves, but it sounded like the Skinners were going to reveal something important. I'm guessing it's about the resort."

"Good work," Trent said, beaming down at her and impulsively kissing her forehead.

Leonard cleared his throat.

"You have to go," Prudence whispered urgently. "I'll see you tonight."

Chapter Nine

Later that same night, Trent gave up trying to sleep. After tossing and turning for more than an hour on the decades-old bed in his stuffy room at the Howatowa Hotel, he pushed himself off the too-hot mattress. As the end of June melted into July and midsummer approached, the evenings stayed balmy until well after dark.

Stripping off his T-shirt, he mopped his face with it and ambled over to the window. He wrestled with the casing that had been long since painted shut and was finally able to throw up the ancient sash. A small breath of slightly cooler night air flirted with his bare skin, smelling of salty ocean spray. Just beyond, the ever-present roar of the sea offered a lullaby to his restless mind.

Even so, he knew he would never be able to get to sleep tonight. And not just because it was so damn hot. No, it seemed that no matter how many sheep he counted jumping the fence, Little Bo-Prudence was always bringing up the rear—usually wearing some skimpy, lacy lingerie. After all, he rationalized, it was hot. Settling his hip against the window ledge, he thought back over their evening together.

They'd decided to meet at her house as usual, in the event that the Skinners were home and the opportunity to spy on them presented itself. Unfortunately, the older couple had been gone for the evening. So, Trent had had no reason to put on a loving, husbandly show for their benefit.

Plus, he figured if he was going to woo her away from Leonard, he was going to have to bide his time. To prove himself worthy. To be a gentleman. Dragging a hand over his mouth and jaw, Trent leaned out the old hotel-room window and inhaled a deep lungful of ocean air.

Tonight, she had cooked the kind of wonderful, home-style meal he'd remembered his own mother preparing when he was a kid. They'd taken their plates and eaten off TV trays out on her tiny balcony, and had watched the waves crash endlessly against the cliffs directly below.

Over dinner, they'd brought each other up to speed on the latest—albeit sketchy—information they'd managed to gather regarding the Skinners' questionable resort plans.

Again, Prudence had reiterated the conversation she'd overheard between the old folks down at the retirement center.

"They were playing poker, just as usual," she told him, picking up her glass of lemonade and pressing its cool surface against her temple. "I stood at the archway, watching for a moment, and that's when I heard Rupert tell them that—" her large green eyes sparkled with the thrill of the chase "—the Skinners were planning a presentation to the community. They want to do it right after the mayor speaks at the pancake breakfast, on the morning of the Summer Festival."

"Refresh my memory," Trent murmured, watching as the beads of moisture from her glass glistened like small crystals in her hair. "I remember going to this thing as a kid. The Summer Festival is only a one-day event, right?"

"Uh-hmm. It's always on the second Saturday of July. It's been that way for years. It's run completely by the seniors for the Howatowa community. They use the money they raise to help fund medical equipment and other necessities for the center. It's always been a great boon both financially and emotionally to the seniors." She smiled her sweet, selfless smile. "They really look forward to making their crafts, and figuring out the games and menus for the children that visit. I loved it as a kid."

"Yeah." Trent nodded and leaned back in the Adirondack chair, propping his feet on the lowest rung of her balcony railing. "I remember the hot dogs and the treasure hunt. It was fun."

"Well, it should be extra interesting this year, if the Skinners show up and make whatever announcement that has everyone so excited," she said, a pensive furrow gracing her brow.

"The second Saturday in July is less than two weeks away," Trent noted, glancing at the date on his watch. "Are the seniors ready?"

"We should be. Everyone has been working like dogs to prepare. Everyone but Leonard, that is," she added ruefully.

A light breeze lifted several strands of Prudence's hair and blew them across her lips. Trent watched in fascination as she pulled the curly tendrils away from her face and lifted the whole wavy mass behind her slender shoulders. Her white, sleeveless camp shirt and shorts contrasted with the silky tan of her smooth skin and Trent swallowed against the sudden longing that filled his belly.

Picking up his own glass of lemonade, he attempted to fill the empty void he felt inside. After a long pull on his drink he said, "So, as soon as the mayor steps down, the Skinners are going to make some kind of announcement?"

Prudence nodded. "Apparently."

"Any idea what they're going to say?"

"Other than the fact that it has something to do with the resort, no. When I stepped into the room, they all froze up like a bunch of little kids caught smoking behind the woodshed."

Trent chuckled.

Lifting her slender shoulders, Prudence curled her bare toes over the railing and looked at him. "I tried to get them to open up, but it was too late. They all hummed and whistled and pretended great interest in their card game. Hetta looked up and acted all surprised to find me standing there. I don't know, Trent, but I almost think that the Skinners have somehow brainwashed all these people. It was eerie. Just like something out of a pod-person-type sci-fi movie."

"Weird," Trent murmured, listening to her story with rapt attention. "I wonder what it means. What did Hetta say when you walked in?"

"Oh...this and that." She ducked her head and ran a fingertip over the rim of her glass.

Trent arched an interested brow. "What is 'this and that'?"

"Oh, you know, stuff like what a nice couple we make, and you know—what beautiful children we'll have." The heat in Prudence's cheeks fled clear down to the tips of her fuchsia-painted toenails. "And, uh, how—" a nervous giggle slipped past her lips "—much we seem to love each other."

"Ah." Trent grinned at her discomfiture. If he didn't know better, he would almost be inclined to think that Prudence cared what he thought about their pseudo relationship. "So, that was all you were able to gather?" he continued, letting her off the hook for the moment.

"Yes." She nodded. "But, that was enough to give me heart failure."

Trent dragged his fingers through his hair, bringing them to his nape where he worked his tense muscles. "I can see why."

"I was going to try to worm some information out of them, but—" her brow puckered "—Leonard came looking for me, and I had to give him a hand with a few things."

"Thank heaven for Leonard," Trent said sarcastically and dropped his arms.

Prudence shrugged. "He's okay."

Earlier that day, Trent had come to the conclusion, as he'd waited for Mart at the State Financial Fraud Section, that Prudence would have to make up her own mind about Leonard. He could tell her until he was blue in the face what a creep Leonard was, but until she saw it for herself, he would just have to bite the bullet. His storming in and kicking Leonard's scrawny butt would never impress a strong-minded woman like Prudence. Especially not when she was under the impression that her relationship with Leonard was divinely inspired.

Now that, he thought, grimacing slightly, was faith.

No. She would have to choose the man she wanted herself. Although, he reflected, feeling the same competitive spirit he encouraged in his students surge in his gut, he didn't plan on making it easy for her to choose Leonard.

"So, what did Mart have to say today?" she'd asked, bringing him out of his reverie.

"Nothing."

"Nothing?"

"Yep." Trent's sigh was filled with frustration. "He couldn't find a single thing on Fantasy Investments. It's almost as if they've never even existed."

Looking perplexed, Prudence stared out at the water. "How odd."

"Yeah. I can't seem to get a handle on any of this wacky scam. Nobody has heard of them. There arc no outstanding complaints filed on them. As far as I can tell, the Skinners don't have a criminal record. I called a private investigator after I left Mart's office. He's says it's likely that Skinner is not their real name, and he's going to do some checking on possible aliases they might be using. But that could take a while...." He slapped the arm of his chair, feeling completely baffled. "This whole thing is driving me crazy."

"Me, too."

When dinner was over, Trent had hesitated outside her front door for a moment, aching to take her into his arms and vent some of his frustration over the dilemma his life had become; to ignore the inevitable and lose himself in one of her kisses. If only to tide him over into his old age, he'd told himself, knowing there was a strong possibility that he would end up losing her.

After all, who was he to emerge victorious over God's obvious greater plan? No. The words "You can't fight city hall" echoed depressingly in his head. And, since the Skinners still hadn't come home, unfortunately, there was no point in kissing her good-night and shouting endearments.

As he'd stood there, opening and closing his fists, there were so many things he wanted to tell her, but knew he could not. Should not. So, instead, he'd given himself one last moment to study her face. He'd seen a brief flash of yearning there, and then, as if she'd willed it away, it disappeared.

Maybe it was for the best.

Maybe Leonard was just the ticket when it came to husband material for Prudence. After all, Leonard would never be caught dead falling through the ceiling and landing on her bed.

Running his hands over his bare chest, Trent backed away from the hotel-room window and forced himself to return to bed. He had to stop thinking about Prudence, or he would lose his mind. As he slipped into bed, his sheets felt clammy and limp, so he kicked them over the edge and flipped his pillow to find the cool spot.

He closed his eyes against the constant, gut-gnawing craving he felt for her, but there she was again, invading his mind, chasing away his sleep. Absently, he wondered if Prudence was having a hard time settling down, as well.

Over the following two weeks, Prudence figured she'd probably slept all of about two hours. She just couldn't seem to get Trent out of her mind. That burning attraction—which had taken her focus off her future with Leonard—coupled with Rupert's sudden interest in a life of crime, had her on the edge of what she feared was a nervous breakdown.

As the last dozen-or-so days had passed, Prudence had almost begun to feel as if Trent lived at her place—and, heaven help her, she was loving it. They spent an incredible amount of time in each other's company, pouring over the clues they'd collected each day and trying to put the pieces of the increasingly bizarre puzzle together. They planned their strategies, filled each other in on the strange comings-and-goings and doings of the odd couple, and generally spent every waking moment that Prudence was not at work, with each other.

Unfortunately, the more time they spent working on this case, the more confused Prudence became. The more she got to know Leonard, the less she liked him. Which was very unsettling, considering how she hated to look a gift horse in the mouth. The more time she spent with Trent, and the more she got to know him as a man, the better she liked him. Now, all the things that used to drive her bananas as a girl, endeared him to her as a woman.

Of course, she mused—as she showered and dressed and prepared for work the Friday morning before the Summer Festival—the fact that Trent took every opportunity to grab her and kiss her senseless didn't help matters at all. She fought her warring emotions over these impromptu kisses the best she could, but, like the folks down at the retirement center, she was beginning to believe the ruse. She, too, was beginning to believe that she and Trent were a couple.

When Prudence looked into her bathroom mirror she saw only a gaunt, sad-eyed shadow of her former self staring back. "Ughhh," she cried, ducking her head into the sink and splashing cold water on her face in an effort to give it some color. Everything was such a mess!

All this waiting and watching was killing her. For, other than waiting for the Skinners to announce their plans at the Summer Festival first thing tomorrow morning, their hands were tied.

They couldn't expose the dastardly plan until there was a dastardly plan to expose. Aside from their speculations about the supposed resort, they still had no hard-and-fast evidence to incriminate the Skinners. For all their weeks of diligent work, they'd come up empty-handed at every turn.

Thank heavens, Prudence thought, Trent had come to town to look into this matter for his uncle. She would never have been able to get through this ordeal by herself. Nor would she ever have felt comfortable confiding in Leonard about any of this. Leonard would have had neither the time nor the patience for such folderol. Again, she had to wonder about his place in her life.

Tiredly, she gathered her hair into a loose knot at the top of her head and began to put on her makeup. With Summer Festival lurking just twenty-four hours away—and a million-and-one things to do before tomorrow morning arrived—it was going to be a long, long day.

Prudence sighed. At least Trent would be there. He'd volunteered to help some Howatowa townsfolk set up several of the larger booths.

A small smile played at the corners of her mouth. Trent was the one reason this day would be even remotely bearable.

Some hours later Prudence stood with Hetta in the retirement center's parking lot, and took a look at the progress being made on the booths for the festival. Suddenly Hetta let out a gasp and Prudence followed the older woman's mesmerized gaze, her mouth going bone-dry.

For there, halfway across the large parking lot, muscles bulging and hammer swinging, worked Trent. And he was a sight to behold. So, Prudence mused, her eyes glazing over much like Hetta's, that's what a football coach looked like without his shirt. My-my, my-my my.

"Oh, my stars," Hetta twittered, adjusting her blouse and throwing her tiny shoulders back. "I think I've just died, Prudence, honey, and gone to heaven." Her smile spread across her face. "Now he," she teased, pointing a fluttery hand at Trent, "could park his shoes under my bed any day." She looked suddenly anxious and glanced up at Prudence. "Don't worry, though, honey. I know he's yours. I'd never steal him."

"Thank you, Hetta. I appreciate that," Prudence said, slipping her arm around the delicate woman's waist.

Norvil chose that moment to hobble by. "Look out, toots," he shouted. "You're startin' to drool." Pausing, he cackled dryly at his joke. "You, too, Prudie," he hollered over his shoulder as he shuffled off.

Prudence and Hetta exchanged pink-cheeked glances.

Hetta pursed her orange lips. "Would you like to punch him, or shall I?"

"I'll leave that honor to you." Prudence smiled, hoping that Trent hadn't caught Norvil's remark.

For the remainder of the afternoon, Prudence tried to avoid letting her gaze wander to Trent, but it was tough. He was everywhere, it seemed, helping to put together the necessary booths, hauling and carrying, lifting and toting, smiling and joking with the rest of the volunteers.

A poignant lump formed in her throat as she watched him flirt with Clementine, teasing the gruff woman into a sunny smile. He had a way of making Norvil feel like a young man again, as—joshing and joking the whole time—the two carried a table across the parking lot. And Hetta. The woman would have driven a saint crazy the way she followed him everywhere, getting under his feet, pelting him with flirtatious questions and telling him stories. Trent seemed not only to tolerate it, but to enjoy it. He really seemed to care for the people she loved so much.

She was going to miss him something fierce when this whole land-scam thing was cleared up and he went back to Seattle to coach his kids and date his woman.

A hot lump seared her throat at the thought of saying goodbye to Trent.

"Trent! Trent!" Breathless and scarlet-cheeked, Prudence came rushing up to where he was putting up the last booth. It had taken much longer than everyone had expected to finish setting up the parking-lot area. It would be dark soon.

Slowly straightening, he squinted into the waning sunlight at her approach. She made such a fetching silhouette against the setting sun, in that gauzy white skirt and pink-and-white-striped sleeveless top. Even with her hair in such disarray, falling out of her normally tidy bun, she looked cool and breezy, like a breath mint. He grinned to himself. Okay, so he was no Longfellow, but she looked terrific, no matter how he phrased it.

"Yeah?" he asked with a rakish smile, at her rather wild-eyed approach. She should relax a little. They had everything under control. He ran a hand across his bare chest, feeling suddenly as if he should be wearing a shirt. He was a hot sweaty slob and she looked so…together.

Well, maybe that was a bit of an overstatement, being that he was looking at her through his rose-tinted glasses.

"Trent!" Panting, she stumbled the last few steps up to him and, clutching his upper arm, labored to catch her breath. "You have to come, quick!"

His heart suddenly stalled. "Why?" he barked, fear of the unknown constricting his throat. "What's wrong? Is it Rupert? Is he okay? Is he sick?" Yanking off his tool belt and hurling it to the ground, he fired questions so rapidly he rendered her completely speechless.

When she had finally caught her breath and was able to speak, she gasped, "He's fine. Physically, nothing is wrong." She increased the pressure of her fingers on his biceps. "But, Trent… Oh my gosh—" her eyes riveted to his with urgency "— the Skinners just got here, and I overheard them say that they want to take Rupert out to see his—" she could barely finish the thought, she was so choked with emotion "—new mansion."

Trent looked around the shadowed parking lot, his heart suddenly beating fiercely in his chest. "What? Isn't it kind of late to be driving all the way out to Howatowa Hill?" he whispered, trying to grasp the meaning of what she was saying. Was this part of the dastardly plot? Were the Skinners going to somehow endanger his gullible uncle?

"They're leaving now! We don't have time to stand here and talk. I'm not kidding!" She tugged on his arm. "Come on, Trent, we have to go find out what's going on. Maybe we can finally figure out what they're up to!"

Trent suddenly launched into motion, following her across the parking lot to the back of the retirement center where, sure enough, a cherry-red minivan sat waiting, the engine running. At the moment, the Skinners and Uncle Rupert were nowhere in sight.

A streetlamp buzzed on overhead.

"Where are they?" Trent demanded, his rigid jaw flexing tightly.

"They're inside talking to a few of the other 'investors' in their resort scam. But, from the way they left the engine running, it looks like they plan on leaving soon." Excitedly, she gestured to the van's back door. "I think we should go, too."

Grabbing her by the forearms, Trent pulled her toward him and looked into her eyes, searching for answers. "You're sure about wanting to follow them? It's getting pretty late."

"Trent Tanner—" Prudence's eyes flashed with eagerness "—after everything we've been through, wild horses couldn't keep me away. This could be our big chance to find out what's happening to Rupert."

For a split second, he just stood there, gazing into her lovely face. Man, how he loved this woman's spunk. Man, he thought, as a wide smile pushed deep dimples into her cheeks, how he loved this woman.

"Okay," he said, reaching for the back door of the van. "This is it. If we get in, there's no way out."

"I don't want out." She looked fiercely up at him.

That settled it, Trent thought, casting a quick glance around the parking lot to make sure the coast was clear.

It was.

Hustling Prudence along, he pulled the lever and opened the

van's back door. They moved inside as fast as humanly possible, and pulled the door shut.

"Trent," Prudence whispered, as they tumbled into the back compartment behind the last bench seat.

"Mmmph," he grunted, wrestling them into the most advantageous position. They had to remain hidden, but at the same time, he thought, struggling for air, they had to be able to breathe. Pulling her body against his, spoon-style, he lifted a greasy old tarp that had obviously been used to change a tire or two, over their heads.

"Ow, uh, Trent," she whispered again, pushing the tarp away from her face.

"Yeah?"

"Maybe we shouldn't close the back door all the way. Just, uh, you know, partway."

"Why?"

"Well, in case we need to make a fast getaway."

Trent thought for a moment. She could have a point. He certainly didn't think the Skinners were capable of causing them bodily harm, but one could never be too careful. And, when it came to Prudence's safety, he wasn't taking any chances.

"Good idea," he said, reaching across her waist and wrestling with the lever on the back door.

"Don't undo it all the way," she squeaked under the heavy weight of his body. "Just open it enough so that we can, uff—" She grunted as he filled her face with his smooth, hard pectoral muscles as he fumbled for the handle. "Just, just open it enough so that it looks closed but we can still—uff, oww—get out if we have to.... Oww!"

"Sorry," Trent apologized, finally getting the door to cooperate, and dragging his chest and belly back over hers. He stilled. "Shh," he cautioned. "Here they come."

The front doors opened and the van rocked with the weight of several passengers embarking and taking their seats. Prudence could feel Trent's ragged breathing puff steadily against her ear. Her heart thudded loudly in time with his breathing. She could hear the Skinners and Rupert speaking in low tones as they fastened their seat belts and made ready to leave.

This was surely the craziest, most exciting thing she'd ever done. And, it had been her idea. Good heavens. She grinned broadly at the wild carefree rapture of it all. How unlike her.

Settling back into Trent's strong embrace, she felt the engine rumble as it was thrown into gear, and the van began to bounce over the parking lot. She just couldn't imagine Leonard ever doing anything this spontaneous. Poor guy. He was missing out on so much that life had to offer.

Well, she thought, her body rolling back against Trent's as Harry Skinner took a sharp corner, she wasn't going to make that same mistake. From now on, she was going to take what life had to offer—sip from the silver goblet, and all of that.

She could only hope that Leonard wouldn't fire her for taking off without his permission.

A tire iron poked her in the knee as Harry took another reckless stab at navigating a curve. Gracious, for an older guy, he drove like a young whippersnapper, she thought ruefully, her head vibrating with every unavoided pothole.

"Oof," she muttered, as the van picked up speed and the G-forces had them sliding toward the rear door.

"You okay?" Trent asked, gripping the bar under the rear seat with one hand and hauling her back up next to him with the other.

"Uh-hmm," she murmured. As long as he was there, holding her that way, she was just swell.

"Good," he whispered, and snaking a protective arm around her waist, he gave her a gentle squeeze.

She twisted around and brought her nose to his. "Can you hear what they're saying?"

"I think that once we get on the main drag, we'll be able to hear better. All these stops and starts here in town are making it hard to hear. Plus, I think Gladys has her window open," he whispered.

Trent had been right. Once they reached the open road, the conversation was much easier to hear.

"Gladys, will ya roll up your window? I'm spending a fortune on gas so that I can air-condition the great Northwest, here," Harry called crabbily over his shoulder. Apparently Gladys was sitting in the back, while the two men occupied the front seats.

"Oh, all right." She sighed, and suddenly the interior of the van ceased to roar. Now Prudence and Trent could hear quite well.

"So," Gladys said, noisily shifting position on the Naugahyde seat, "it looks like everything is all set for tomorrow." She laughed. "Trent and Prudence are still in the dark, huh?"

"Yep," Rupert crowed. "And, as far as I can tell, we've pulled the wool over the eyes of that Leonard idiot, too."

Harry snorted. "Criminy sakes, if anyone could mess up our plan, that little jerk could." Stomping on the gas, the driver threw his passengers back, then forward as he punched the brake. "Yeah," he continued. "I'd like to see about getting rid of that guy." His voice was ominous.

"I don't know, Harry. I don't think you should go that far. He's a jerk, yes," Rupert agreed with a laugh, "but he's not that bad."

"Whatever," the other man griped. "I still think everything would run a lot smoother without him there to screw everything up. The sooner he's out of the picture, the better, as far as I'm concerned."

"I have to agree with Harry," Gladys added.

Twisting around, Prudence grabbed Trent's hands and gripped them tightly. Eyes round as full moons, she stared up into his face and saw the beginnings of her own horror mirrored there in the darkened interior of the van.

"They want to kill Leonard?" she whispered to him under the stifling confines of the dirty old tarp. How horrible.

Trent gave his head a slight shake. "I don't know. It sure sounds like it, doesn't it?" He held her tightly.

"Oh, Trent," Prudence moaned softly, nearly paralyzed with fear, "what are we going to do?"

"I don't know, honey. Just try not to panic."

They traveled for a few more minutes before the van lurched violently and swung to the left as Harry merged onto the old gravel road that led to where the mansion sat on the hill, overlooking the sea. The old house—which for years all Howatowa schoolchildren believed was haunted—stood on a cliff by itself a good seven or eight winding miles away from town.

Even if they'd thought to bring a phone and had been able to dial 911 for help, help would be a long time in coming, Prudence thought worriedly. Perhaps hopping in the van with Trent and following Rupert and the Skinners out to Howatowa Hill hadn't been such a brainy idea, after all.

"Slow down, will ya, Harry?" Gladys barked. "You're killing me, back here."

"I gotta make good time, if I'm going to get there while there's still enough light to show Rupert the answers to his questions. Just sit tight, Gladys. We're almost there."

"Gladys—" this was from Rupert "—before I throw all my time and money into this project I need to make sure of a couple of things."

"Okay, fine." Gladys sounded more than a little disgruntled at being tossed about so unceremoniously.

"She should try riding back here with us," Trent muttered.

Alternately punching the gas and stomping on the brake, Harry navigated the narrow road that hugged the cliff.

A sheer drop, roughly five hundred feet straight down, flanked the little van's rotating wheels mere inches from the vehicle's left side. No guardrail had ever been installed, as the old, pothole-filled road was so seldom used. Swerving suddenly, Harry jumped on the brake, then, as if fearing he might get stuck—or worse, topple over the edge—he leaped on the gas.

"Harry!" Gladys shouted. "For pity's sake. Watch what

you're doing! The back door just swung open, and I think something rolled out.''

"Quit yelling, Glad," Harry ordered huffily. "Criminy sakes, this road is murder."

"Well, aren't you going to stop and see what rolled out?" she demanded.

"We don't have time. We can get it on the way back."

"I don't think so."

"Why not?"

"Because I think it went over the cliff."

"No big deal," Harry said. "It was probably just that old tarp. And a tire iron."

Chapter Ten

"Trent!" Prudence screamed and crawled as fast as her long skirt would allow, over to where he lay sprawled against a scraggly fir tree. As she glanced down the sheer precipice, a sudden wave of nausea swept over her. In the fading daylight, she could barely make out the ocean as it crashed against the jagged rocks that jutted from the shoreline far, far below.

Thank God for the patch of trees that sprouted from the cliff's edge. If it hadn't been for their sturdy trunks, she was sure that both she and Trent would have been goners by now.

"Trent, oh, Trent," she panted, tears streaming down her face. Staying as far away from the edge as she dared, she reached out and took his face between her hands, patted his cheeks, whispered endearments to him and begged him not to die. Locating his wrist, she pulled it into her lap and stared through blurry eyes at the second hand on her watch. His pulse was strong, she noted, able to perform her job as a nurse in this crisis, even though she was more than just a little emotionally involved with the patient.

She didn't think she could go on living if anything should ever happen to Trent.

"Wha-what happened?" he asked muzzily, slowly opening his eyes and looking up at her. His face wore a dazed expression.

Prudence let out a sob of relief. "Oh, thank God you're all right," she sniffed, wiping her running eyes and nose on her soiled skirt. "We fell out of the van," she said in needless explanation, as she rocked back on the heels of her white summer sandals and inspected him for lumps and bumps.

"So, I see," he returned ruefully, brushing some gravel off one of the burning scrapes that now graced his naked torso. "For a second, there, I thought I was falling through your ceiling again." His grin was lopsided.

"Remind me to buy you a crash helmet for Christmas," she scolded, as her eyes skittered to the sheer drop less than a yard from where they sat. Once again, the realization of the fate they'd just managed to escape assailed her. Light-headed, she began to chatter like a magpie. "You scared me half to death for a minute, there. How are you feeling? Is anything broken? Don't move until you're sure nothing is broken. Do you think you can move?"

"Slow down, woman," Trent groaned, and gripping an exposed tree root, he slowly levered himself to a sitting position. "I can't think when you're pelting me with questions that way."

He was beginning to sound like the Trent she knew and loved. "Sorry," she said, and extended her hand to him. "Here, let's get away from the edge. I'd feel a little better if we weren't hanging out over the cliff this way."

"Killjoy," he teased.

Taking his hand in hers, she very carefully helped him scoot a few feet toward the relative safety of the road. Using each other as support, they slowly stood and assessed the damage.

Prudence pulled a few twigs out of the bun that sagged loosely at the back of her head and smoothed her torn and stained skirt back down over her legs. "Are you going to be all right?" she asked worriedly.

"I think so," he said, wincing. "Man. That really knocked the wind out of me." He touched her elbow. "How about you?"

"I don't think anything is broken. Actually, I think I'm going to be fine. I, uh…think I landed on you," she admitted and gave him a wobbly, watery grin.

Sniffing again, she knew that she was still feeling quite shaken up. After all, it wasn't every day that she fell out of a moving vehicle—driven by homicidal maniacs—and nearly plunged to her death. Not to mention the fact that Trent seemed to be bleeding in several places. Reaching out, she lightly ran her fingertips over one of his larger scrapes, then proceeded to probe his ribs.

"Eee—yiii," he gasped and clutched her hand. "That smarts."

"Sorry," she murmured, stepping closer. "You wouldn't have gotten so scraped up if you'd had a shirt on," she observed, studying his body in the fading light. "You're going to have some pretty painful spots for a while. We should probably see about getting you cleaned up as soon as possible." She glanced around. "Any ideas where we should go from here?"

Trent hobbled to the middle of the road and looked about. "Well…" he said, thoughtfully rubbing his brow, "since neither of us seems to need an emergency room, I vote that we proceed with our original plan."

"You mean follow the Skinners." She sighed. That plan no longer seemed quite so tantalizing, considering what they'd overheard.

Trent nodded. "I really don't see that we have much choice. It will be dark in about ten minutes or so, and I don't know about you, but I don't want to walk all the way back to town, in the pitch-black—" he jerked a thumb toward the cliff behind him "—especially at this height."

"I guess you're right. Although," she said, falling into step with Trent as he began ascending the steep road that led to

Rupert's new house, "I'm not sure which is worse—walking home, or riding with old Harry, there."

"No lie," he snorted. Taking her hand in his, Trent led her around a pothole. "Have you ever ridden with anyone who punched the gas and brakes that way?" he asked, sending her an incredulous look. "I'm surprised they both don't wear permanent neck braces."

Somewhere in the dark woods above them, an owl hooted. Prudence jumped and tightened her grip on his hand. Between the wild animals and the haunted house and the sordid Skinners, her nerves were strung tighter than one of Hetta's sweaters. A dog howled and she shrieked.

"Hey, shh, easy there," Trent whispered, pausing for a moment and cupping her cheeks between his hands. He kissed her forehead and held her while she pulled herself together. "We don't want the bad guys to know we're here, right?"

"Right, right, right," she agreed, the whispered words coming in short puffs. She wished they could forget the Skinners and stand there for the rest of the night, holding each other. She didn't want to go any farther. Trent's steady heartbeat beneath the smooth, warm wall of his chest was so comforting. Couldn't they just pull up a stump and take a load off? Relax? Call it a night?

Keeping her close to his side as they worked their way up the hill, Trent murmured soothing words.

"Don't be afraid. Nothing is going to hurt us. Come on," he said, his low, steady voice meant to encourage. "We're only a few city blocks or so from the top of the hill. Then we can hopefully avoid being detected by the Apple Dumpling Gang—"

Prudence giggled a short, nervous hiccup.

"And find out what they're up to. I have a feeling they're already parked and looking around by now. If there isn't any electricity up there—and I doubt there is—then they probably won't be staying long. So," he said, picking up speed, "we need to hustle."

Prudence stretched her steps to match his leggy stride.

Trent continued outlining his plan in a low voice. "We'll go straight to the van, hide in the back and sneak a ride to town with them. If we're lucky enough to figure out what their plan is, we can go to the police tonight."

"That's a good idea, although I have to tell you I'm not looking forward to finding out what the...plan is," Prudence lamented.

"I know."

Feeling slightly winded as they began to half jog up the steep hill, she said, "Well, whatever happens, we can't let them address the community tomorrow at the Summer Festival."

"Right." A glint of determination flashed in his eyes as he looked down at her.

"Too many people have been taken in by them already. I hate the idea of the little festival being invaded by those crooks." Prudence clutched at the painful stitch in her side.

"Me, too," Trent said, his voice a strange mixture of grim sadness. "Don't worry. We'll stop them. No matter what," he assured her, "we'll stop them before they can get Uncle Rupert into any more trouble."

They suddenly halted as they crested the hill and the magnificent old house loomed into view.

"Wow!" Prudence murmured, completely amazed. "I've never seen the place this close up before."

"Me neither," he admitted. "As a kid, I only ever saw it from the road below."

"It's huge," she whispered, awed by the enormous, dark structure. Its imposing silhouette towered against the cloud-streaked evening sky, as they stood craning their heads back to take in the full, chilling picture. "It's ten times bigger than it looks from the road."

"Yeah," he agreed. "Looks like something straight out of *Psycho*."

She groaned. "You would have to mention that."

"Come on." Touching her elbow, he indicated for her to follow him around the perimeter of the overgrown grounds.

Even in the twilight, Prudence could see that at one time, the landscaping had been magnificent. An old statue rose eerily in the center of a fountain that stood in the middle of a rose garden surrounded by the circular drive. Rhododendron bushes gone wild and neglected box hedges still lent a rustic elegance. No wonder Rupert was so excited. In its heyday, the house must have been worth a mint.

As they fought their way through the underbrush, the murmur of voices reached their ears.

"Yeah," Harry was saying as they paused several yards away and peered at him from the depths of the thicket. "I think you might be on to something, Rupert, old boy. If you can con your little friends down at the retirement center into going along with this, then you'll have it made in the shade. Easy street, buddy."

"That's what I thought!" Rupert cried jubilantly. "I thought you'd see it my way."

"I don't know," Gladys said dubiously. "Seems kind of risky to me. And, what about Leonard? He makes me nervous. I get the feeling he's on to us. He's a troublemaker, that one."

"That wimp?" Harry's heavy jowls quirked in annoyance. "Forget him, Glad. I told you. We'll figure out a way to get rid of him."

Prudence gasped.

"Harry," Gladys asked, sounding somewhat nervous, "did you hear something?" Her razor-sharp eyes darted rapidly around the yard. "Something over there?"

"Gladys, when aren't you hearing something?" To Rupert, Harry said, "She is convinced that someone is hiding out in our attic, listening to everything we say."

Prudence and Trent exchanged wide-eyed glances.

Rupert chuckled.

"I'm not kidding, Harry," Gladys insisted, her voice taking on a fevered pitch. "It sounded like it came from over there."

She pointed to the bushes where Prudence and Trent were huddling.

Prudence gasped again.

"There it is again!" the older woman squealed.

"Probably just a wild animal. No big deal," Harry assured her.

"Big deal or not, I'm ready to go. This place is giving me the creeps. Come on, Harry. Let's not drive down that spooky hill in the dark. It's too darn dangerous. I want to go home while there is still a little light. Now!" Gladys ordered, setting into motion and rushing toward the van. With an agility that contradicted the snow-white of her hair, she leaped inside as though the hounds of hell were after her.

"Women," Harry grunted in an effort to seem as if the possibility of unexpected visitors didn't bother him in the least. However, the haste with which he followed his wife belied his bravado. Rupert wasn't far behind and after hopping inside, Harry gunned the engine and shot out of the driveway and down the hill.

Openmouthed, Prudence and Trent stared after their last chance at transportation to town.

"Trent?" Prudence's voice was breathy as the realization that they were stuck on Howatowa Hill—in the dark, no less—sank in.

Grasping her hands in his, he pulled her to her feet and led her out from behind the brush where they'd been hiding. He slipped his hand around her waist and brought her up against his side.

"Don't panic," he said. "Give me a minute here, and I'll think of something."

Prudence allowed her head to thud against his bare chest. "You're going to need more than a minute to get us out of this mess," she lamented. "I'm afraid we're stuck."

Looking around, Trent spotted an old cast-iron bench, whose curlicued gingerbread was in dire need of a paint job. "Come on over here," he instructed, deciding that if he sounded masterful and in control, he would begin to feel that way. Because, as it was, he was feeling hungry, tired, chilly, sore and mad as hell at the people who'd just driven away. Tugging Prudence down next to him on the bench he said, "We should probably figure out what our options are."

"Options?" she asked dully. "What options?"

"Well, I guess we could walk home tonight. Or—" he ran a hand over the gooseflesh that was beginning to form on his arms "—at least down to the road. We could probably hitch a ride back to town from there."

"I thought you didn't like the idea of going back down that treacherous driveway." Prudence shook her head. "No, we've already flirted with death on that cliff once tonight. Let's not push our luck."

"I could go and get a car and come back for you," he volunteered.

"No!" She gripped his arm and shot a look of sheer terror back at the empty house. "Don't leave me here alone." Her eyes were pleading.

"Prudie, the house really isn't haunted."

"It isn't?" Her voice was small as she stared up at the gargoyles that leered down at her. She could swear that Norman Bates was peeking at her from behind the curtains in one of the upstairs windows. "That's not what all the kids used to say. Oh, Trent, please don't leave me."

Leaning down, he kissed her forehead. "Don't worry, honey. I won't do anything you don't want me to. Listen," he said, slapping at his chest, "the mosquitoes are eating me alive. Why don't we go inside?"

"I don't want to."

"Aww, jeez, Prudie. Give me a break. I'm half naked here, and these bugs are enjoying the buffet that my wounds are providing. Besides—" he looked up at the heavy clouds that scudded across the sky, occasionally obliterating the moon-light "—I'm getting kind of cold." He shivered as if to prove his point.

"It's probably not very warm in there," she argued.

"True, but it's probably not windy, either." He slapped at a droning insect that had landed on his neck.

Looking at him through the dim light of the full moon as it peeped between the clouds, she had to agree. It was rather cool out here. But, at least they were alive, she thought, sending a dubious glance at the upstairs window where the imaginary Norman lurked.

"Okay," she conceded, against her better judgment. "I'll go in. But, you have to promise that if the ghost shows up, we get to come back outside."

Trent grinned. "Deal."

It seemed that actually getting inside the old relic was easier said than done. They first tried all the doors, and found them locked. Then they advanced to all the lower-level windows— basement and then first story—to no avail. Finally they agreed that since climbing up to the second story would most likely yield the same results, they would forgo venturing on the rickety trellis.

So, Trent picked up a rock, and doing as little damage as he possibly could to the window in the back door, was able to unlock the dead bolt and allow them to slip inside.

All the while, Prudence hovered behind him like a second skin. Her hand rested lightly at the small of his bare back, and her breath warmed a spot just between his shoulders at the nape of his neck. He grinned to himself as he entered the old house and stood blinking in the dark, in an effort to orient himself. This getting-stranded thing was becoming rather enjoyable. He had a feeling that she didn't even realize that they were joined at the hip this way.

Unfamiliar with the floor plan of the house, Trent could only guess that this had been some kind of servants' entrance in the past. Together, they moved as one unit through the shadowed rooms, the only sounds being the wooden floorboards that creaked and groaned beneath their cautious footsteps, and the mutual thunder of their heartbeats.

Moving from room to room, they battled the cobwebs and tried not to let the childhood stories of horror on Howatowa Hill fill their minds.

"I think this must have been the library, at one time," Trent whispered into Prudence's ear, then wondered why he was whispering.

Moonlight shivered into the room from behind the racing clouds, revealing row after row of empty shelves, which stared down at them from the unusually high walls. Once their eyes adjusted to the lack of light, they could see that the room was octagonal in shape, and the ceiling was domed with a giant chandelier hanging imposingly from its center. An empty fireplace, sporting a heavily carved marble mantel, gaped in a sinister fashion from across the room. The sparse furnishings were hidden from view by large white drop cloths.

"That looks like it might be a couch of sorts, over there by the fireplace. Maybe we should spend the night in this room," Trent said, noting that Prudence was shaking like an aspen leaf in a stiff breeze. Suggesting that they explore upstairs would probably be asking too much.

She nodded dumbly, still clutching his arm in a death grip. "This room is fine."

"Okay, since that's settled, why don't I go see about getting us some water from the kitchen? I need to wash up a little after my fall."

"No!" Prudence hissed in a terrified stage whisper. "I mean, yes, let's go get you cleaned up, but I'm going with you."

After an emotionally harrowing trip back through the house, they finally located the kitchen near the servants' entrance. Unfortunately, the plumbing—for whatever reason—was not functioning, and there was no water to be had. Prudence was forced to concede that waiting to clean Trent's wounds was probably safer than hitching back to town. Dodging imaginary horrors, she threaded her fingers through Trent's belt loops and hung on for dear life as he led her back to the room in which they'd chosen to spend the night.

They tiptoed across the library floor to the antique settee. Pulling the dust-filled drop cloth around their shoulders, they sat curled as closely together as the old piece of furniture would allow, sharing what little body warmth they were able to generate between them.

"It almost feels as if it's going to rain," Prudence whispered, watching the branches of an ancient oak tree tap the window, like beckoning fingers of doom.

"I hope not," Trent muttered, pulling her even closer.

"You know, I saw a movie once, where this couple was trapped in an old, haunted house, kind of like this one..." she said absently.

"And?"

"And, they didn't make it out alive."

"Well—" Trent's chest rumbled with low laughter "—isn't that a pleasant thought."

As if she hadn't heard him, Prudence continued, "The old pipe organ started to play—" her eyes grew wide "—all by itself! And then, the eyes in the family portraits began to follow them from room to room, and then—" she looked up at him, and clutched his strong arms with fearful fingers "—the walls began to bleed!"

"Sheesh, Prudence. Would you can it? You're giving me the willies."

"You can't get the willies."

"Why not?"

"Because," she said, darting a nervous look around for bleeding walls, "that's my job."

Trent's stomach rumbled in noisy protest at having been neglected for so long. "I'm hungry," he whispered. "I haven't eaten since lunch."

"Me, too," Prudence agreed, relaxing her grip on his arms. "Starved."

"I wonder if there's anything to eat around here." Still

whispering, Trent looked over the silent, eerie room, as if there might just happen to be a cheeseburger and a side of fries waiting for him on one of the empty shelves. "I guess not," he said with a disappointed sigh.

Prudence reached into her pocket and withdrew a small bag of peanuts. "You're in luck," she said, handing him the bag.

"All right!" Trent whispered jubilantly and kissed her temple. Tearing it open, he poured himself a handful and handed the rest to her. "You know," he said thoughtfully, tossing a nut into his mouth, "I think I might have a pack of breath mints in my pocket, for dessert."

"Dare we dream?" Prudence murmured with a grin. "You know, I'll bet that when the lights are on, this place isn't really as bad as all the kids said it was, back in grade school. The marble and mahogany and crystal alone are worth a fortune. And—" she slanted a glance up at Trent from where she sat nestled against his shoulder "—I can see why your uncle thinks there might be some value here."

Trent harrumphed. "What's he gonna do with this giant pile of fancy brickwork? No way he can take care of it." He shook his head. "Naw, value or no, he's been conned. Big time."

"Mmm," Prudence hummed, slowly chewing her peanuts, one at a time to make them last. "Well, anyway, I'm not nearly as scared as I thought I'd be..." she continued, proud of herself. Something popped loudly in the next room. "What was that?" she demanded in a choked whisper. Half climbing into Trent's lap, she wrapped her arms tightly around his neck.

Grinning, Trent peeled her grip away from his throat. "Would you relax? It's just the house settling."

"Oh." Drawing her face out of his neck, she dared a quick peek around the room. "I thought it might be...him."

"Him who?"

"You know. Him. The old guy who died in this house. The one—" she lowered her voice and brought her lips to his ear "—the one that *haunts* this place. Remember?" Leaning slightly back, she peered though the dusk into his face.

"No." Trent shook his head. "You must have heard a different story than I did."

"You didn't hear about the guy who killed himself by jumping out of the attic?" At Trent's noncommittal shrug, she continued, "Everyone says that he was a really old, really—" again she lowered her voice "—ugly, really, really rich guy." Her eyes were as round as the moon that hovered outside the window. "Anyway, he married this really young, really beautiful, really, really poor girl. And they lived here together, and he wouldn't let her go anywhere by herself because he was—" she lowered her voice again "—insanely jealous."

Shifting to a more comfortable position, Trent stroked Prudence's soft, midnight hair and smiled. Yes, indeedy. This evening was turning out to be a lot more fun than he'd ever imagined.

Moonlight reflecting in her eyes, she went on with her tale. "I guess there used to be a gatehouse down at the start of the driveway, because one day, the really old guy went down there and caught his wife in the arms of a really young, really handsome, really, really hunky guy."

She wiggled her eyebrows at Trent for emphasis, and he laughed. Then, before she could go on, he pulled her across his chest and cradled her in his arms. "Continue," he commanded, resting his palm on her flat stomach. Mmm, he thought with an inward sigh of contentment, he couldn't think of anywhere he would rather be, scrapes and all.

"And so, legend has it that he locked them inside and set the gatehouse on fire. Then, because he was so sad, he ran to the attic to watch it burn and then, just before the firemen could get up the hill, he jumped to his death." Prudence's sigh was filled with romantic drama.

Trent snorted. "That sounds like the girlie version to me."

Rolling her cheek against the warm firm wall of his chest, she looked up into his eyes. "Oh?" She sent him a cheeky grin. "What story did you guys come up with?"

"Well," Trent mumbled, popping the last of his peanuts

into his mouth, "the way I heard it, a band of robbers broke into this house and stole a treasure." He thoughtfully stroked his chin. "Jewels, I think."

"Jewels?" Prudence pinched her lower lip between her fingers. "Do you think Rupert knew about that? Maybe that's what he was showing the Skinners."

Trent thought for a moment, then shook his head. "Naw. Anyway, as the robbers were making their escape, they got into a fight over who was going to get what, down by the gatehouse, and when they were done fighting, they had burned down the gatehouse and everyone was dead. And, on nights when the moon is full, you can still smell the smoke and hear the dead guys running around, clanking chains and stuff."

"Wouldn't you know, tonight would have to be a full moon?" Prudence moaned. "I don't like that story. It's...gross."

"That's gross? I suppose a flaming affair and a flying old, ugly, rich guy are a lot less gross."

"No." She grinned at him. "Both stories are rather maudlin, and most likely not a bit true."

"Kids." Tipping his chin to his chest, he smiled down at her.

"Yeah. Kids."

For a moment, they smiled into each other's eyes, remembering.

Prudence nibbled her lower lip pensively before she was finally to speak. "Trent?"

"Hmm?"

"How come you used to torture me all the time in grade school?" She looked down at her hands and twisted her birthstone ring around in circles on her finger. "Did you hate me?"

He inhaled deeply, causing her head to loll against his supporting arm. He'd wondered when she would ever get around to asking that. From the look on her face, screwing up her nerve to ask had taken some doing. He guessed it was time to fess up and tell the truth. Exhaling the breath he'd been holding, he decided to bite the bullet.

"It's not what you think," he began, absently threading his fingers through her hair. "I didn't hate you at all. In fact, it's just the opposite. Most of the catastrophes that happened to you, especially in the eighth and ninth grade, happened because I had a huge crush on you."

Rearing back, Prudence opened her mouth into a slack, disbelieving grin. "No way."

"As God is my witness." He held up a solemn hand.

"You mean to tell me that you give the girl you have a huge crush on a bouquet of poison oak and stinging nettle?"

"I didn't know that's what it was! I swear, Prudie. I just thought they were pretty. I was kind of hoping to get a kiss for all my effort, but instead you ended up crying and going home and, man—" he sighed, looking suddenly vulnerable and boyish "—I felt like a first-class louse."

Prudence's skeptically narrowed eyes softened some. "Okay, what about the skinned hogshead in my backpack?"

Trent laughed at the memory. "Okay. I'll admit that was really bad judgment on my part. I should have known that a sweet little girl wouldn't be quite as impressed with that sort of thing as I was. But, hey, I thought for sure I was going to earn us an A-plus for that baby on our biology-lab final. I was positive, when I was swiping it from the trash heap, that you would throw yourself into my arms and kiss my face off out of gratitude." He looked at her ruefully. "Again, I had it figured all wrong."

Prudence covered the smile that threatened the corners of her mouth with the back of her hand as she looked up at him. "What about my hair?" Reaching up, she touched his fingers as they twined in her tresses. "You always made so much fun of my hair."

Trent frowned. "I never made fun of your hair," he protested. "I loved your hair. I couldn't keep my hands out of it." He let his fingers sift through her soft locks. "I still can't." His eyes dropped to her lips. "I guess I figured that if I couldn't get you to throw yourself into my arms and kiss me, I'd have to settle for tugging on your curls as often as possible."

"Oh," she whispered and ducked her head shyly. He'd wanted her to kiss him back in grade school? That was the last thing she'd have guessed.

From there, the conversation turned to how life in Seattle had differed from life in the little town of Howatowa. They brought each other up-to-date with stories of their high-school years, reminisced about friends and acquaintances long forgotten, and discussed their hopes and dreams for the future.

Then, once again, as midnight passed and the hours ticked toward morning, the conversation traveled back to their childhood and together they wandered down memory lane with smiles and laughter. Neither one was conscious of the bond that had been forming between them as it continued to grow stronger. Like the tender roots of a young tree, strengthening their hold on solid ground, these were the common threads that inexorably bound Trent and Prudence to each other.

Prudence sighed with relaxed contentment against the warmth of Trent's bare chest and stomach. Closing her eyes, she thought back to the freckle-faced rascal who had plagued her youth, and giggled softly.

"What?" Trent murmured, his cheek nestled against the top of her head.

"You sure expected me to throw myself at you and kiss you a lot, back when we were kids."

She felt his cheek lift as he smiled. "A boy can dream, can't he?"

"Mmm." Prudence nodded. Her hair made a rasping sound as she tilted her head back from from his whiskered jaw. "I guess I owe you." She slanted a heavily lidded gaze into his moonlit eyes.

"What?" His voice was low and sexy.

"A few hundred kisses."

The corners of his mouth tipped lazily. "True. And, I'm thinking it's about time I collected."

"Mmm." She sighed, as she lifted her face to his.

From the moment their lips met, there was no more pretense. There were no neighbors, no senior citizens, no more reasons to perform. The kiss was as sweet and full-bodied as a fine wine, and the intoxicating side-effects had Prudence reeling with thoughts and feelings and emotions that she'd never experienced before.

"You have no idea," Trent whispered against her mouth, cradling her head firmly in his hands, "how I used to dream about doing this very thing back in school."

That knowledge sent a surge of unprecedented joy ringing throughout her body. Trent had wanted her. And, from the looks of things, he still did. Suddenly, she felt happier than she could ever remember feeling before in her life. "Really?" she murmured, searching his face for the truth. He had wanted to kiss a plump little wallflower such as herself? But why?

His blue eyes became a smoldering black in the darkened room. "Oh, yeah…" he whispered into her mouth. "All the time." And, as he pushed her lips apart with his, he proceeded to bridge the years, to heal the hurts, and to fill her heart.

Threading her hands into his soft blond hair, she moved closer to him and allowed the kiss to happen. To wash over her like the waves that crashed against the shore down below. It was perfect.

So why, she wondered, even as she was losing herself to the ecstasy of Trent's touch, did she have the guilty feeling that she would never be able to feel this kind of passion for Leonard? Because, Lord help her, she didn't want Leonard. It didn't matter anymore that he was heaven-sent. Just as it didn't matter that he had dark curly hair and large green eyes.

She hoped that she would be forgiven for returning her gift, because there was no way that she and Leonard were a decent fit.

For the rest of her life, Prudence was sure that when she

paused to envision the man of her dreams, he would have silky blond hair, a smoothly shaven face and laughing blue eyes.

"Ohhh," she moaned, partially because of the fix she was in, and partially because of the fire that Trent was setting in her mouth, her jaw, her neck and the hollow of her throat. This was so horrible. This was so wonderful. This was so horribly wonderful.

Their breathing became strident, labored. Prudence felt sure that her lungs might explode from the way her heart was slamming around inside her chest. She felt herself being swept more firmly onto Trent's lap and against his chest, then sinking with him toward the arm of the little settee where they settled in a tangle, like the vines of the ivy that climbed the side of this house.

Prudence couldn't be sure when the first wispy fingers of smoke tickled her nose, penetrating her muzzy, passion-fogged mind. Stilling in Trent's arms, she pulled her mouth slightly away from his and spoke. "Trent?"

"Hmm?" he asked, nuzzling her cheek and temple with his nose.

"Do you smell smoke?"

He chuckled softly. "Definitely," he said, claiming her mouth again.

"No," she said urgently, tearing her lips reluctantly from his. "Really. I smell smoke. As in fire."

He frowned for a moment before sitting bolt upright, taking her with him. "Yes." He quickly nodded. "I smell it, too."

Prudence's nose collided with his as she clung to his chest and urgently whispered into his ear. "You don't suppose it's that full-moon-jewel-robber-smoke that you guys used to talk about as kids, do you?"

"I don't think so.,.."

"You're probably right," Prudence squeaked, beginning to panic. "Plus, I don't hear any chains clanking."

"No," Trent agreed grimly, prying her hands from around his waist and standing. "But I do hear something suspicious coming from the back of the house.... And if I'm not mistaken—'' he was thinking out loud now as he began to move swiftly toward the back door ''—that's where the smell of smoke is coming from.''

"No, Trent," Prudence called, her voice scarcely above a whisper as she began to hyperventilate. "Don't...ahh...go in...ah...there!''

Not wanting to follow Trent, but wanting even less to be left behind, she started after him, arriving in the kitchen just in time to see him tackling someone as a small pile of newspaper burned merrily in the softening darkness. As the flames shot higher, Trent and what looked like a man in a ski mask, rolled around on the floor, fighting.

Was it the ghost of the old owner? she wondered briefly. No. This man was very real. And very dangerous. Prudence didn't know how to help Trent, but she knew she had to do something.

Acting on sheer adrenaline and instinct, Prudence ripped off her formerly gauzy white circular skirt and began beating at the quickly spreading flames.

Chapter Eleven

Stumbling around in the smoke-filled room, Prudence listened with half an ear to the sounds of men engaged in furious combat as she single-handedly fought the fire. Then, after much hullabaloo, it grew silent and Trent staggered out of the haze to lend a somewhat bruised and bloodied hand. Together, they were finally able to put the fire out.

Thinking quickly, Trent had yanked down the drapes in the dining room and smothered the little remaining fire Prudence hadn't already handled with her skirt. As she sagged wearily against the doorframe, Prudence eyed the charred mess that littered the old tile floor. Thankfully tile didn't burn that easily. Probably another reason the house hadn't gone up like a box of matches.

"Who do you suppose that was?" she asked, lifting her eyes from the floor to Trent. He was covered from head to toe with streaks of soot. She could only imagine that she looked exactly the same. In what was surely a futile effort to tidy her appearance, she tucked a stray wisp of hair back into her sloppy bun.

He shrugged. "Don't know. He got away before I could

pull his mask off. I guess I was a little preoccupied, worrying about you playing fire fighter that way...." He let his sentence trail off tiredly.

"Who would do such a thing?" she wondered aloud. And why would it happen the same night that Rupert and the Skinners were here poking around? It didn't make any sense. Why would they want to burn down the house that they were all crowing so happily about only hours before? There had to be another reason. "Do you think it was just a schoolboy prank?"

"I don't know." Trent's hand wandered to the swollen cheekbone under his right eye. "I can tell you this, though. That guy was no schoolboy. He wasn't a ghost, either."

"Oh, Trent," she murmured, pushing away from the doorframe and crossing the room to once again assess the damage. "Following the Skinners has become decidedly bad for your health." Reaching up, she gently cupped his bruised cheek in the palm of her hand.

"Are you kidding?" he growled, slipping his arms around her waist and hauling her close. "I wouldn't have missed last night for a million dollars."

"Really?" she whispered.

"Really," he promised, and kissed her firmly on the mouth before he set her away from him so that he could check her condition. "How about you? Are you all right?"

"Well..." Smiling wanly, she looked down at what was left of her skirt. The waistband held fast to a few remaining shreds of singed fabric, and looked much like a grass skirt after a skirmish with a lawn mower. A fire-breathing lawn mower. "After a hot shower and a decent meal, I'm sure I'll be fine."

"I guess we should consider ourselves lucky," Trent said with a teasing twinkle in his eye. "Between the two of us, we have an entire outfit." His eyes roved appreciatively over her bare legs, now that they were nearly completely revealed due to the ridiculously shredded skirt.

"Maybe we could start a trend," she quipped, feeling her mood lighten slightly at his good-natured words.

Grinning, he unsuccessfully attempted to rub a little of the soot from the tip of her nose. His eyes traveled to the window, and watched the gradually lightening sky for a moment. "Do you have enough energy to start home?" he asked, darting a concerned glance down at the skimpy sandals she wore.

Inhaling deeply, she shrugged. As much as she hated to stay, she hated to go. She wouldn't have missed last night for a million dollars, either.

"We should probably get going," Trent said. "It's already getting pretty late."

Prudence looked at her watch and gasped. "Oh, no! It's already seven o'clock. The mayor is scheduled to speak during the pancake breakfast at eight. The Skinners are on after that!"

"Well, let's get a move on. If we're going to make it in time to stop them, we're going to have to get the lead out." Striding across the room, Trent moved to the back door and looked expectantly at her. "What are we waiting for?"

Shoulders slumping, she slogged over to him. "A taxi?" she asked in a small, defeated voice, suddenly realizing that they would never make it in time. Not even if the taxi was jet-propelled. "Trent, there's no way we can make it."

"Sure, we can. Come on. I'll teach you how to hitch."

"Oh, sure. Who in their right mind would pick us up?" She guffawed rudely, as they began their descent down the steep driveway together. "You look like you just competed in a sewer-landfill-swamp triathlon. And won."

"Oh, yeah?" Trent's laughter echoed off the hilltops. "Well, you look like you lost."

Prudence's laughter rose to the sun-dappled peaks with his. "Good grief, Trent," she gasped, when she could speak without howling, "we can't go to the Summer Festival looking like this."

"True," he quipped. "One look at you and Harry is going to know you've been cooking again."

* * *

As the mayor—smiling broadly all the while from his perch on the old gazebo-covered bandstand—pontificated about the amazing financial future of the flagging community, which was "nothing less than a miracle!" Trent and Prudence jumped off the back of a still-moving hay truck and flew like demons possessed toward the pancake-eating crowd.

"Stop!" they shouted, holding dirt-streaked hands and running hell-bent for leather to where the mayor stood, somewhat nervously watching their approach.

A low murmur began to rumble through the crowd. Ladies gasped. Men stood. Children giggled and pointed.

With Trent's help, Prudence hoisted herself up onto the stage in a most unladylike fashion, and then turned and gave him a hand as he leaped up beside her.

"Stop, oh, please, please, stop!" she pleaded, rushing up to the mayor and clutching his hands in hers.

The mayor blinked for a moment, and then peered through the soot and grime, the scrapes and bruises and tangled mass of hay-filled hair. "Prudence Mackelroy?" he asked, his dumbfounded voice screeching and reverberating with feedback as he thundered his surprise into the P.A. system. "Good gracious, where have you been?" His gaze flew to Trent. "What on earth happened to you?" he demanded. "We expected you hours ago."

Another gasp rippled across the stunned crowd.

"Yes," she panted, clutching Trent's arm for support. "Please, if I may have a moment, this is an emergency."

"Ahh, bu-but," the mayor sputtered at the unusual turn of events.

Not waiting for his reply, Prudence scanned the crowd and quickly picked out the Skinners. "There they are," she cried, pointing at the elderly couple, where they stood at the edge of the stage, waiting to be introduced to the crowd.

Harry and Gladys Skinner exchanged perplexed glances.

"Don't listen to those two!" Prudence warned, sagging back against Trent's strong, soothing presence. She'd never been more wound up in her entire life. She knew that if it hadn't been for him, she would never have had the courage to say what needed to be said. "Whatever you do, don't listen to anything these two swindlers have to say!'' She pointed dramatically at the Skinners. "They are running a phony land scam. The resort they're promising is nonexistent!"

The crowed collectively gasped.

Trent squeezed her arm and nodded. He spotted Uncle Rupert in the front row. "They've already taken in several of our good citizens," Trent added. "That's why they're here this morning. To con the rest of you out of your precious savings."

"Phony land scam?" the mayor roared, his face turning beet red. "Will somebody please tell me what's going on here?" He gestured to the pink and white balloons and the festive signs. "I don't know anything about any swindlers! I thought Mr. and Mrs. Skinner were here on behalf of the senior center to throw you a surprise engagement party."

Prudence suddenly paled beneath her soot-blackened face as she took in the sight before them. For everywhere, just as the mayor had said, were signs that read: Best Wishes Prudence and Trent, Happy Engagement!

What on earth was going on? Prudence wondered, feeling faint.

Unable to grasp the meaning of this curveball or dodge the curiously staring eyes, Prudence looked at Trent and they both simply smiled in humiliation at the gaping crowd, and waved.

A short while later, after his meeting with the fire chief, Rupert led the bedraggled couple into the retirement center. "Coffee?" he offered with a sympathetic grin. At their negative response, he held the door to Prudence's office open and ushered them inside. Closing the door behind them, he gestured for them to take the two chairs situated in front of her desk, and he settled himself behind it.

Prudence felt like a little kid suddenly, seated in the principal's office, waiting for a reprimand. She'd never been so embarrassed in her life. Catching her reflection in the mirror behind her desk, she cringed and sank down in her seat. Never in a million years would she live this morning down. Her gaze fell to her lap. Try as she might, she couldn't get the few remaining scraps of her skirt to cover much of anything, so she gave up, hung her head, and waited for the lecture to begin.

Because she was starting to fear that if the scandalized looks on the faces of the entire population of Howatowa were any indication—she and Trent had missed the boat at some point during their sleuthing escapade.

Tenting his fingers under his chin, Rupert propped his elbows on the desk, pursed his lips thoughtfully and studied the disheveled couple. "I guess it's time someone filled you two in on what's going on around here."

"I would appreciate that," Trent said humorously, his steely eyes riveted to his uncle.

Sighing heavily, Prudence nodded in agreement.

"Okay," Rupert said. "Forgive me as I backtrack a little bit for you. I don't know what you kids know and don't know, so I'll spill the whole story."

"Fine." Trent bobbed his head curtly.

Rupert's chair squeaked comfortably as he settled in to tell his tale. "First of all, I want to make it perfectly clear the Skinners aren't con artists. Or swindlers. Or whatever else you kids have gotten it into your heads that Harry and Gladys are up to." He scratched his temple and looked askance at them.

"I've known Harry Skinner since I was a kid," he told them. "We went to school together at the same grammar school you kids attended. And, even after Harry married a local girl and moved away, we kept in touch. Gladys was a couple grades behind me and Harry in school. Sweet girl. Gladys Howatowa, one of the few remaining original descendants of Chief Howatowa, of the Howatowa tribe." He inclined his head at Trent and Prudence. "You must have studied the Howatowans in history class."

At their nod, Rupert continued. "Anyway, Harry and Gladys moved away and ended up making a fortune together in the cookie industry, of all things. You've probably eaten their cookies before. Grandma Skinner's Famous Cookies? They have a store in practically every mall in the country."

Dumbfounded, Trent and Prudence could only nod and stare at Rupert.

"Poor Gladys," Rupert said. "As lucky as they were in business, Harry and Gladys were never fortunate enough to have a child of their own. You know, I think that's why they palaver so much attention on that mutt of theirs..." he reflected. "Anyway, since they never had any heirs to pass their fortune to, and since they aren't getting any younger, they decided they needed to start dealing with their money now." Rupert leaned forward and tapped on Prudence's blotter with one of her pencils. "Kids, the Skinners are rich. Filthy rich. Multi-multimillionaires. But, you'd never know by looking at them, or by the way they live. They are two of the most down-to-earth folks you'd ever want to meet."

Prudence slumped in her chair and buried her flaming face in her hands. Trent—looking decidedly uncomfortable—swallowed, and cast his eyes to the floor.

"So, they formed Fantasy Investments, a secret little company, to act as an anonymous benefactor to help boost Howatowa's sagging economy. Since they have no family to call their own, with the possible exception of Willard—" Rupert chuckled "—they decided to adopt our townsfolk—many of whom are descendants of Chief Howatowa's tribe, like Gladys—and distribute their inheritance while they were still alive and could see it do some good.

"And, since they are senior citizens themselves, they are partial to the folks here at the Howatowa Retirement Center, and have allowed these people to invest first—" he looked sternly at the young couple "—*before* the word leaked out—in the huge proposed resort, designed to put the town back on its feet. The seniors are getting into the deal for pittance, and the percentages they earn will put them on easy street for life."

Trent ran a hand over his aching forehead and eyes. "Uncle Rupert, what about the house you supposedly won, up on Howatowa Hill? What's all this about you having to pay the back taxes and other costs?"

Rupert grinned. "I won that house in a poker game with

Harry. I cheated, of course, and he knows it but doesn't care. Still, I insisted on paying the taxes and transactions costs. It only seemed fair.'' The old man stretched and stuck Prudence's pencil behind his ear.

"I thought you told me that you won it in a raffle," Trent argued.

"Did I say that?" Rupert asked innocently. "Well, I may have padded the truth a little, boy. I don't go around telling everyone how I cheat at cards. People who don't understand may lose respect for me." He grinned rakishly. "Anyway, I have an idea to turn that old place into a fancy new retirement center, with my earnings from the resort. This place—" he looked around Prudence's office "—is falling apart, and we're going to have to move someday anyway. The resort will be going in up on the Howatowa Hill. So, I figured why not move us all out to where the action is? All-new, up-to-the-minute medical equipment, a bigger staff, with a—ahem—" he cleared his throat and tried to wipe the distasteful look off his face "—a new director. Harry and I figured that since we were going to end up owning the retirement center, we'd hire somebody we liked to direct this place."

"Is that what you were talking about, when you and the Skinners were saying how you wanted to get rid of Leonard?" Prudence blurted out.

Rupert stared at her, perplexed. "How did you know about that?"

"Uh-oh." She looked at Trent for help. "A little birdie told me?" she squeaked feebly.

"Why do you want to get rid of Leonard?" Trent wondered aloud, diverting the man's curious gaze from Prudence.

"Well." Rupert ran his tongue over his lips. "Before today, we wanted to get rid of him, simply because he was such a mean-spirited, rotten little creep." He looked at Prudence. "Everyone misses Rodney Pillson."

Trent grinned broadly at that, and Prudence allowed her head to drop to the back of her chair. Was she the only one who hadn't seen Leonard's defects? Exhaling, she recrossed her legs and again futilely tried to arrange the tiny scraps of singed fabric farther over her thighs. No, if she was going to be really honest, she'd known something was wrong with Leonard from the very beginning. She'd just been blinded by the fact that he had dark curly hair and a mustache, like her father.

"However," Rupert continued, "after speaking to the fire chief a moment ago, it would seem that we have good reason to dismiss Leonard." Trent's uncle smiled gratefully at them. "Some Good Samaritan called the fire department this morning and reported a little fire up at the mansion."

Trent averted his eyes. He'd borrowed the hay-truck driver's phone and reported the fire in hopes of catching the arsonist.

"And luckily," Rupert said with a happy grin, "the police were able to arrest Leonard before he skipped town."

"What?" Prudence's jaw dropped.

Rupert clicked his cheek. "Yep. It would seem that he caught wind of our plan to expand without him, and he went up to the house last night and tried to burn it down. They found his wallet in the kitchen. Guess he was kinda mad at us."

"Leonard?" Prudence gasped, shocked. The masked man who tried to burn down the haunted house was Leonard? How could she ever have been stupid enough to believe that Leonard was the answer to her prayer? Prudence was afraid she was going to be sick. The Skinners were innocent.

Dear God, how could she and Trent have made such a mess of everything? How could they have made such fools of themselves? How could she ever face the fine folks of Howatowa ever again? Her mind reeled and reverberated with questions and answers, with humiliation—and anger. Anger at herself for being such a suspicious boob, and anger at Trent for getting her involved in this sordid mess in the first place.

"So!" Rupert slapped his hands in finality on the desktop. "That answer all your questions?"

"I guess so." Trent nodded, and pulled the corners of his mouth into a self-deprecating smile.

"Mmm," Prudence muttered, closing her eyes.

"Good," the old man said. "Because I have a few questions of my own. Where the heck were you kids this morning, anyway? Sweeping chimneys? On second thought, don't tell me. I don't want to know." He looked them both over from head to toe and laughed a deep, rumbling belly laugh. "You can tell me all about it another time. Anyway, you know, Gladys went to a lot of time and trouble to organize your little engagement party. When she found out you kids were going to be getting married, she got so excited." Rupert pulled the pencil from behind his ear and pointed it at them. "She's been working on your party plans day and night for weeks now. So, go put in a quick appearance out there on your way home."

Prudence wanted to curl up and die. The poor woman. Working so hard and for what? It was all a lie. She sent a murderous glance at Trent.

"Well, okay, then." Rupert scooted his chair away from the desk. "You kids can stop worrying about us gray-hairs now, you hear? We've been around the block a couple of times, and, whether you believe it or not—" he directed this to Trent "—we can take care of ourselves."

The old man stood and slowly walked to the door. "I've got a bingo game to run, and some explaining to do on your behalf. I'll catch you both later, after you've had a chance to—" he chuckled "—freshen up." With that, he shuffled out, closing the door behind him.

The days of speculation, coupled with a sleepless night and a healthy dose of humiliation proved to be more than Prudence could take.

Sniffing, she sat stiffly in her chair and stared pointedly at Trent. "I can never show my face in this town again, and it's all your fault," she accused heatedly.

"*My* fault?" He lifted an arrogant brow. "Oh, so now I'm the one who sullied your reputation, is that it? Well, who the hell was that wild woman standing next to me on the podium a few minutes ago, huh?"

She inhaled sharply, outraged. "I never would have thought that my sweet little neighbors were swindlers if it hadn't been for you!"

"Oh, yeah? Whose idea was it to follow them up to the house in the first place? Yours! And, I nearly got myself killed in the process, thank you very much."

They were now standing nose-to-nose, shouting wild recriminations, blaming each other for the morning's fiasco.

As their voices escalated, Prudence wanted to stop, to throw herself into Trent's strong arms and cry. Cry over the fool she'd made of herself, cry over the fact that now that they knew the truth, he would be leaving Howatowa and going back to his life in Seattle. The tears that had been brimming at the edges of her lashes finally gave way and spilled down her cheeks, leaving whites streaks in the soot as they fell.

She could just kill him. The time—which she had managed to successfully ignore for weeks, now—had finally arrived. He was leaving and she was crying. But not because he wasn't staying to help bear the brunt of their humiliation, but because she would miss him more than she could bear.

"Oh, yeah," she retorted. "That's just fine for you to say. You get to leave this town and go back to your job in Seattle. You don't have to stay here and face these people and try to hold your head up."

What, she wondered frantically, was she saying? Just like when they were kids, the argument had stopped making sense. She wasn't telling him how she really felt at all. She should be stepping into his arms and telling him that she'd managed to fall in love with him, in spite of the color of his hair.

Tired, defeated and beaten to a pulp, Trent just stared at her as she ranted. Before he could begin to tell her how much he loved her and wanted to marry her and make that set of twins with her, he needed about three uninterrupted hours of sleep, a hot shower, and a waist-high stack of pancakes from the griddle that was still sizzling away, just outside the window. Holding up his hands, Trent turned and strode to the door.

Afraid he would say something he would regret, he simply told her, "I'll see ya around," and left.

Staring after him through tired, blurry, tear-filled eyes, Prudence collapsed into her chair and had a good cry over her bleak future. No husband, no father to her twins, and—now that the Skinners were going to co-own the retirement center—most likely, no job. Leaning over her bare lap, she held her head in her hands and cried as though her heart would break.

.   That evening, after a fitful nap, a bracing shower and a hot meal that she'd forced past the searing lump in her throat, Prudence ventured to her front porch and knocked tentatively on the Skinners' front door. Gladys answered with a smile.

"Rupert thought you might stop by," she chirped. "Come in, dear, come in."

Prudence gazed at the tiny woman whom she now recognized from the cookie package and wondered how she'd ever mistaken the sweet face for that of a criminal.

"Oh, Mrs. Skinner," she began, dabbing at her swollen eyes with a tissue. Her emotions were still so raw. She'd lost so much today. Her dignity, her future, and…Trent. "I just came by to beg your forgiveness. I'm—" she sniffed and sobbed "—so sorry about the mix-up. It's just that we were so concerned for Rupert and the folks down at the retirement center. We meant well, we really did."

"I know, honey," Gladys said, folding the young woman in a motherly hug. "Rupert told us everything."

"He did?"

"Uh-hmm. He and Harry had lunch with Trent this afternoon. I guess Trent really blames himself for the whole mess." She chuckled warmly. "Feels pretty foolish about not trusting his uncle and so forth. I must tell you, though, Harry and I haven't had such a laugh for years." Eyes twinkling, she patted Prudence on the back and led her to a chair. "Rupert told us how he fell through your ceiling, dear. Oh, boy, did Harry howl at that. Trying to convince us that you two were swinging from the light fixture. I never could quite bring myself to believe that." She giggled. "Anyway, I don't want you to waste another minute crying over this, you hear? The mayor got quite a chuckle over the whole thing, and ended up explaining to everyone that your crazy appearance during his speech this morning was all part of the plan."

"He did?" Prudence asked, beginning to relax slightly, and see the humor in the ridiculous situation. "Mrs. Skinner, I also wanted to thank you for the engagement party you worked so hard on." Prudence's lower lip began to tremble. "I'm just sorry it was all for nothing."

"What do you mean, honey?"

"Trent and I were never really going to get married. It was all just another one of our horrible lies. I'm sorry," she whispered. Sorry for her lies, and sorry that she and Trent really weren't engaged.

"Not going to get married?" Gladys cried. "Oh, now, honey, you must be mistaken about that. Why, that boy loves you with all his heart! It's obvious! If I didn't know better, well, I'd think he was heaven-sent, just for you."

The doorbell rang before Prudence could ask the woman what she meant.

"Just a moment, dear," Gladys said as she stepped to the front door.

"Hello, Mrs. Skinner." Prudence could hear Trent's voice from where she sat in the living room. "I just stopped by to extend my sincere apologies over the horrible mistake we made this morning," he continued as the elderly woman led him into her home.

"Oh," Prudence said, feeling suddenly shy around Trent. She didn't want him to see her red-rimmed eyes and tear-stained cheeks. "I'll just leave you two alone," she said, shielding her face on her way out the door. "Thank you, Mrs. Skinner, I'll come back when it's more convenient."

"But, dear," Gladys called, to no avail. Prudence had already gone.

Back in her apartment, Prudence sagged against her door

and let the tears fall. It was so painful to look at him, knowing that he would soon be leaving and taking her heart with him.

Swiping at her eyes with her sleeve, her watery gaze traveled to the hole in her bedroom ceiling. Gladys had said, "If I didn't know better, I'd think he was heaven-sent, just for you." Could she be right? Prudence wondered, a small spark of hope beginning to burn in her breast.

Just because he didn't have curly black hair didn't mean anything. And, good heavens, Seattle wasn't that far away.

Maybe, just maybe, Trent *was* the answer to her prayer. Slowly, a sense of peace began to fill her heart. For, if there was one thing she knew for sure, when something was meant to be, it was meant to be.

The doorbell rang, startling her. Adjusting her clothes and smoothing her hair, she pulled open the door. Her eyes widened with surprise. "Trent?"

"Gladys sent me."

"She did?" That Gladys really was an angel.

"Uh-hmm." Trent grinned.

"Why?"

"She said she wanted me to come over here and comfort my bride."

Prudence sniffed and dimpled slightly. "She said that?"

"Yep." His smiling eyes were filled with hope. With joy. With love.

"What'd you say?"

"I told her that there was nothing on earth I'd rather do." He took a step into the foyer and pulled her into his embrace, gently shutting the door behind him. "But, I guess before I do that, I have to do one thing."

"What's that?"

He led her into the living room and, settling her into a chair, knelt to face her. "Ask you to marry me."

Prudence's heart leaped joyfully into her throat. Was he serious? "Are you sure you want to do that?" Reaching out, she caressed the bruise below his eye with her fingertips.

"You may not live to tell the tale, the way we seem to generate trouble."

He grinned and shrugged. "Honey, I've never been more sure of anything in my life." Bracing himself with his hands on her knees, he leaned forward and touched his nose to hers. "I've waited for, and dreamed about, this moment ever since the ninth grade," he murmured, his lips mere inches from hers.

"The ninth grade?"

"Okay, the fifth. Prudence Mackelroy," he whispered, with a tender smile, "will you marry me?"

Her brow wrinkled with worry. "But, what about your job in Seattle?"

"Well, considering the job that Harry Skinner offered me at lunch today," he said, regarding her from under lazily hooded eyes, "I'll be resigning my teaching position."

Her eyes grew round with shock. "Harry offered you a job?"

Trent grinned that old Trent-the-Terror grin she'd come to know and love. "Yep. He said he'd never seen anyone so committed to the welfare of others before in his life. He was so impressed, he told me he wants me to run the resort's accounting department."

"No," she breathed in awe.

"Yes!" Trent's eyes twinkled happily. "And, don't go telling that I blabbed, but he wants you to direct the new retirement center." He kissed the backs of her hands. "So. Will you marry me?"

Mirth bubbled into Prudence's throat at the irony of the situation. "Trent, back in the ninth grade, my prayers were answered when you packed up and moved out of town." She giggled at his pouty lip. "Little did I know that this many years later, my prayers would be answered when you came back. Mr. Tanner, I would love to marry you."

"Hallelujah and amen to that!" Trent whispered, just before he pulled her into his arms and covered her mouth with his.

Epilogue

Prudence leaned back against the pillow of her hospital bed and smiled. From where she sat, she could hear Trent out in the hallway, passing out cigars to the group that had come to wish them well.

"Clementine," she could hear Trent saying in a hushed voice. "Here's an extra one, just for you. Cuban."

Clementine's raspy laughter reverberated down the hallway. "You're going to make a great dad, kid. A great dad."

"Won't he, though?" Hetta trilled. "And, so handsome. My stars."

"Watch it, toots," Norvil groused, teasingly. "You're droolin'."

"I guess this would make me a great-uncle, huh?" Rupert wanted to know.

"Why, yes, Rupert," Gladys said, a hint of longing in her voice. "I guess it would."

"Gladys," Trent asked, "you know anything about changing diapers?"

"Yes, honey, I've changed a few nappies in my time."

"Good. Because we're going to keep you busy."

"Oh, how wonderful," she exclaimed, obviously delighted. "Isn't that wonderful, Harry?"

"Mmmph," Harry grunted. "Wonderful."

Wonderful. Prudence smiled sleepily and had to agree. Life was simply wonderful. Each and every one of her prayers had finally been answered.

All of her friends up at the new retirement center were well and happy and considerably wealthier than they had been last year at this time.

The resort was up and running and the local economy was booming.

But, best of all, Prudence had her husband, whom she loved with all her heart.

And, to enhance that perfect love, she had just this morning been blessed with twins. MaryJane and John, named for her late parents. And they had blond hair, and laughing blue eyes....

Just like she'd always wanted.

*   *   *   *   *

Silhouette's newest series

YOURS TRULY

Love when you least expect it.

Where the written word plays a vital role in uniting couples—you're guaranteed a fun and exciting read every time!

Look for Marie Ferrarella's upcoming Yours Truly, *Traci on the Spot*, in March 1997.

Here's a special sneak preview....

1

Morgan Brigham slowly set down his coffee cup on the kitchen table and stared at the comic strip in the center of his paper. It was nestled in among approximately twenty others that were spread out across two pages. But this was the only one he made a point of reading faithfully each morning at breakfast.

This was the only one that mirrored *her* life.

He read each panel twice, as if he couldn't trust his own eyes. But he could. It was there, in black and white.

Morgan folded the paper slowly, thoughtfully, his mind not on his task. So Traci was getting engaged.

The realization gnawed at the lining of his stomach. He hadn't a clue as to why.

He had even less of a clue why he did what he did next.

Abandoning his coffee, now cool, and the newspaper, and ignoring the fact that this was going to make him late for the office, Morgan went to get a sheet of stationery from the den.

He didn't have much time.

Traci Richardson stared at the last frame she had just drawn. Debating, she glanced at the creature sprawled out on the kitchen floor.

"What do you think, Jeremiah? Too blunt?"

The dog, part bloodhound, part mutt, idly looked up from his rawhide bone at the sound of his name. Jeremiah gave her a look she felt free to interpret as ambivalent.

"Fine help you are. What if Daniel actually reads this and puts two and two together?"

Not that there was all that much chance that the man who had proposed to her, the very prosperous and busy Dr. Daniel Thane, would actually see the comic strip she drew for a living. Not unless the strip was taped to a bicuspid he was examining. Lately Daniel had gotten so busy he'd stopped reading anything but the morning headlines of the *Times*.

Still, you never knew. "I don't want to hurt his feelings," Traci continued, using Jeremiah as a sounding board. "It's just that Traci is overwhelmed by Donald's proposal and, see, she thinks the ring is going to swallow her up." To prove her point, Traci held up the drawing for the dog to view.

This time, he didn't even bother to lift his head.

Traci stared moodily at the small velvet box on the kitchen counter. It had sat there since Daniel had asked her to marry him last Sunday. Even if Daniel never read her comic strip, he was going to suspect something eventually. The very fact that she hadn't grabbed the ring from his hand and slid it onto her finger should have told him that she had doubts about their union.

Traci sighed. Daniel was a catch by any definition. So what was her problem? She kept waiting to be struck by that sunny ray of happiness. Daniel said he wanted to take care of her, to fulfill her every wish. And he was even willing to let her think about it before she gave him her answer.

Guilt nibbled at her. She should be dancing up and down, not wavering like a weather vane in a gale.

Pronouncing the strip completed, she scribbled her signature in the corner of the last frame and then sighed. Another week's work put to bed. She glanced at the pile of mail on the counter. She'd been bringing it in steadily from the mailbox since Monday, but the stack had gotten no farther than her kitchen. Sorting letters seemed the least heinous of all the annoying chores that faced her.

Traci paused as she noted a long envelope. Morgan Brigham. Why would Morgan be writing to her?

Curious, she tore open the envelope and quickly scanned the short note inside.

Dear Traci,
I'm putting the summerhouse up for sale. Thought you might want to come up and see it one more time before it goes up on the block. Or make a bid for it yourself. If memory serves, you once said you wanted to buy it. Either way, let me know. My number's on the card.
Take care,
Morgan

P.S. Got a kick out of *Traci on the Spot* this week.

Traci folded the letter. He read her strip. She hadn't known that. A feeling of pride silently coaxed a smile to her lips. After a beat, though, the rest of his note seeped into her consciousness. He was selling the house.

The summerhouse. A faded white building with brick trim. Suddenly, memories flooded her mind. Long, lazy afternoons that felt as if they would never end.

Morgan.

She looked at the far wall in the family room. There was a

large framed photograph of her and Morgan standing before the summerhouse. Traci and Morgan. Morgan and Traci. Back then, it seemed their lives had been permanently intertwined. A bittersweet feeling of loss passed over her.

Traci quickly pulled the telephone over to her on the counter and tapped out the number on the keypad.

*   *   *   *   *

Look for TRACI ON THE SPOT
by Marie Ferrarella, coming to
Silhouette YOURS TRULY
in March 1997.

In the tradition of
Anne Rice comes a
daring, darkly sensual
vampire novel by

MAGGIE SHAYNE

BORN IN TWILIGHT

Rendezvous hails bestselling Maggie Shayne's vampire
romance series, WINGS IN THE NIGHT, as
"powerful...riveting...unique...intensely romantic."

Don't miss it, this March, available
wherever Silhouette books are sold.

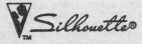

MILLION DOLLAR SWEEPSTAKES
OFFICIAL RULES
NO PURCHASE NECESSARY TO ENTER

1. To enter, follow the directions published. Method of entry may vary. For eligibility, entries must be received no later than March 31, 1998. No liability is assumed for printing errors, lost, late, non-delivered or misdirected entries.

   To determine winners, the sweepstakes numbers assigned to submitted entries will be compared against a list of randomly, preselected prize winning numbers. In the event all prizes are not claimed via the return of prize winning numbers, random drawings will be held from among all other entries received to award unclaimed prizes.

2. Prize winners will be determined no later than June 30, 1998. Selection of winning numbers and random drawings are under the supervision of D. L. Blair, Inc., an independent judging organization whose decisions are final. Limit: one prize to a family or organization. No substitution will be made for any prize, except as offered. Taxes and duties on all prizes are the sole responsibility of winners. Winners will be notified by mail. Odds of winning are determined by the number of eligible entries distributed and received.

3. Sweepstakes open to residents of the U.S. (except Puerto Rico), Canada and Europe who are 18 years of age or older, except employees and immediate family members of Torstar Corp., D. L. Blair, Inc., their affiliates, subsidiaries, and all other agencies, entities, and persons connected with the use, marketing or conduct of this sweepstakes. All applicable laws and regulations apply. Sweepstakes offer void wherever prohibited by law. Any litigation within the province of Quebec respecting the conduct and awarding of a prize in this sweepstakes must be submitted to the Régie des alcools, des courses et des jeux. In order to win a prize, residents of Canada will be required to correctly answer a time-limited arithmetical skill-testing question to be administered by mail.

4. Winners of major prizes (Grand through Fourth) will be obligated to sign and return an Affidavit of Eligibility and Release of Liability within 30 days of notification. In the event of non-compliance within this time period or if a prize is returned as undeliverable, D. L. Blair, Inc. may at its sole discretion, award that prize to an alternate winner. By acceptance of their prize, winners consent to use of their names, photographs or other likeness for purposes of advertising, trade and promotion on behalf of Torstar Corp., its affiliates and subsidiaries, without further compensation unless prohibited by law. Torstar Corp. and D. L. Blair, Inc., their affiliates and subsidiaries are not responsible for errors in printing of sweepstakes and prize winning numbers. In the event a duplication of a prize winning number occurs, a random drawing will be held from among all entries received with that prize winning number to award that prize.

5. This sweepstakes is presented by Torstar Corp., its subsidiaries and affiliates in conjunction with book, merchandise and/or product offerings. The number of prizes to be awarded and their value are as follows: Grand Prize — $1,000,000 (payable at $33,333.33 a year for 30 years); First Prize — $50,000; Second Prize — $10,000; Third Prize — $5,000; 3 Fourth Prizes — $1,000 each; 10 Fifth Prizes — $250 each; 1,000 Sixth Prizes — $10 each. Values of all prizes are in U.S. currency. Prizes in each level will be presented in different creative executions, including various currencies, vehicles, merchandise and travel. Any presentation of a prize level in a currency other than U.S. currency represents an approximate equivalent to the U.S. currency prize for that level, at that time. Prize winners will have the opportunity of selecting any prize offered for that level; however, the actual non U.S. currency equivalent prize if offered and selected, shall be awarded at the exchange rate existing at 3:00 P.M. New York time on March 31, 1998. A travel prize option, if offered and selected by winner, must be completed within 12 months of selection and is subject to: traveling companion(s) completing and returning of a Release of Liability prior to travel; and hotel and flight accommodations availability. For a current list of all prize options offered within prize levels, send a self-addressed, stamped envelope (WA residents need not affix postage) to: MILLION DOLLAR SWEEPSTAKES Prize Options, P.O. Box 4456, Blair, NE 68009-4456, USA.

6. For a list of prize winners (available after July 31, 1998) send a separate, stamped, self-addressed envelope to: MILLION DOLLAR SWEEPSTAKES Winners, P.O. Box 4459, Blair, NE 68009-4459, USA.

Silhouette ROMANCE™

COMING NEXT MONTH

#1210 MYSTERY MAN—Diana Palmer
Our 50th Fabulous Father!
Fabulous Father Canton Rourke was in Cancun, Mexico, to relax
with his preteen daughter, but damsel-in-distress Janie Curtis was
putting an end to that mission. The perky mystery writer was looking
for a hero able to steal hearts—would Canton prove the perfect
suspect?

#1211 MISS MAXWELL BECOMES A MOM
—Donna Clayton
The Single Daddy Club
Confirmed bachelor Derrick Cheney knew nothing about raising his
young godson—but the boy's teacher, pretty Anna Maxwell, was the
perfect person to give him daddy lessons. Problem was, she was also
giving Derrick ideas to make Miss Maxwell a mom...and his wife.

#1212 MISSING: ONE BRIDE—Alice Sharpe
Surprise Brides
Stop that bride! When groom-to-be Thom Powell went to track
down his runaway fiancée, maid of honor Alexandra Williams
reluctantly came along. But as the marriage chase went on, Thom
began wondering if his true bride might be the one riding right beside
him....

#1213 REAL MARRIAGE MATERIAL—Jodi O'Donnell
Turning Jeb Albright into a "respectable gentleman" would
definitely be a challenge for Southern belle Mariah Duncan.
Especially when this strong, rugged Texan had the lovely Mariah
thinking he was real marriage material...just the way he was!

#1214 HUSBAND AND WIFE...AGAIN—Robin Wells
Love and marriage? Divorcée Jamie Erickson had once believed in
the power of both. Then Stone Johnson, her handsome ex-husband,
returned, reawakening memories of the happiness they'd shared, and
setting Jamie to wonder if they could be husband and wife...again!

#1215 DADDY FOR HIRE—Joey Light
Jack was glad to help out single mom Abagail with her children. His
little girl needed a mommy figure as much as her sons needed a male
influence. But Jack soon realized he didn't want to be just a daddy
for hire; he wanted the job forever—with Abagail as his wife!

As seen on TV!
Free Gift Offer

With a Free Gift proof-of-purchase from any Silhouette® book,
you can receive a beautiful cubic zirconia pendant.

This gorgeous marquise-shaped stone is a genuine cubic
zirconia—accented by an 18" gold tone necklace.

(Approximate retail value $19.95)

Send for yours today...
compliments of ▼ *Silhouette*®

To receive your free gift, a cubic zirconia pendant, send us one original proof-of-purchase, photocopies not accepted, from the back of any Silhouette Romance™, Silhouette Desire®, Silhouette Special Edition®, Silhouette Intimate Moments® or Silhouette Yours Truly™ title available in February, March and April at your favorite retail outlet, together with the Free Gift Certificate, plus a check or money order for $1.65 U.S./$2.15 CAN. (do not send cash) to cover postage and handling, payable to Silhouette Free Gift Offer. We will send you the specified gift. Allow 6 to 8 weeks for delivery. Offer good until April 30, 1997 or while quantities last. Offer valid in the U.S. and Canada only.

Free Gift Certificate

Name: _____

Address: _____

City: _____ State/Province: _____ Zip/Postal Code: _____

Mail this certificate, one proof-of-purchase and a check or money order for postage and handling to: SILHOUETTE FREE GIFT OFFER 1997. In the U.S.: 3010 Walden Avenue, P.O. Box 9077, Buffalo NY 14269-9077. In Canada: P.O. Box 613, Fort Erie, Ontario L2Z 5X3.

FREE GIFT OFFER
ONE PROOF-OF-PURCHASE

084-KFD

To collect your fabulous FREE GIFT, a cubic zirconia pendant, you must include this original proof-of-purchase for each gift with the properly completed Free Gift Certificate.

084-KFD

Silhouette Romance proudly invites you
to get to know the members of

The Single
Daddy Club

a new miniseries by award-winning author
Donna Clayton

Derrick: Ex-millitary man who unexpectedly
falls into fatherhood
MISS MAXWELL BECOMES A MOM (March '97)

Jason: Widowed daddy desperately in need of some live-in help
NANNY IN THE NICK OF TIME (April '97)

Reece: Single and satisfied father of one about
to meet his Ms. Right
BEAUTY AND THE BACHELOR DAD (May '97)

Don't miss any of these heartwarming stories as
three single dads say bye-bye to their bachelor days.
Only from

Silhouette ROMANCE™

In February, Silhouette Books is proud
to present the sweeping, sensual new novel
by bestselling author

CAIT LONDON

about her unforgettable family—*The Tallchiefs.*

TALLCHIEF FOR KEEPS

Everyone in Amen Flats, Wyoming, was talking about
Elspeth Tallchief. How she wasn't a thirty-three-year-old
virgin, after all. How she'd been keeping herself warm at
night all these years with a couple of secrets. And now one
of those secrets had walked right into town, sending
everyone into a frenzy. But Elspeth knew he'd come for
the *other* secret....

"Cait London is an irresistible storyteller..."
—*Romantic Times*

Don't miss TALLCHIEF FOR KEEPS by Cait London, available
at your favorite retail outlet in February from

Silhouette®

Look us up on-line at: http://www.romance.net

CLST